the
metapheromenoi

Brendan Connell was born in Santa Fe, New Mexico, in 1970. His works of fiction include *Unpleasant Tales* (Eibonvale Press, 2013), *The Architect* (PS Publishing, 2012), *Lives of Notorious Cooks* (Chômu Press, 2012), *Miss Homicide Plays the Flute* (Eibonvale Press, 2013), *Jottings from a Far Away Place* (Snuggly Books, 2015), *Cannibals of West Papua* (Zagava, 2015), and *Pleasant Tales* (Eibonvale Press, 2017).

brendan connell

the
metapheromenoi

THIS IS A SNUGGLY BOOK

ISBN: 978-1-64525-025-8

The slightly different version of the first 27 chapters of this book
were previously published as *The Metapheromenoi: Book I, Deserotes*
by Mt. Abraxas Press, in 2018. Chapters 28-108 are original to the
current volume.

the
metapheromenoi

1.

If I was not already quite certain before I commenced with the operation, the look on his face when he saw me would have plainly unveiled the game that he had been playing.

"Oh, hello," he said with an unpleasant cadence to his voice. "I am just here for a cleaning."

"I'm going to clean your teeth."

"Don't you usually take care of more serious things? I was under the impression that it was Leaena's job to do the cleanings."

I put a bib around his neck and told him that Leaena was out sick and that I would be taking care of him. He did not conceal his disappointment very well. Considering that she and I were already engaged, considering that we were soon to be wed as man and wife, I must say that it was very unwise of him to be such a poor dissembler. I suppose he thought that, since I was a smallish, un-muscular sort of man, I was also a harmless fool. Small men are routinely underestimated.

In any case, I started to fool around inside his mouth with my Cooley Pic, buttering his ears all the while with the usual small talk that patients find both pleasant and relaxing. I asked him how his photography was going, not in the least wanting him to answer, but knowing full well that he couldn't say a great deal with seven of my fingers crowding his mouth. He clucked and grunted and closed his eyes.

I began to work off the amalgam from his upper left second premolar. I poked it savagely a few times with my pic. He winced and looked up at me.

"A little tender, eh?"

He nodded and tried to speak.

"Shhh," I said. "Nothing to be alarmed about."

I gave him a reassuring smile, looked at his chart and then went back into his mouth and rooted around for a few minutes.

He was becoming visibly uneasy and several times tried to speak. I put down my pic and let him spit into a plastic cup.

"Ivan," I said, "there seems to be a bit of a problem with your upper left second premolar. Looking at your chart I can see that you had a class II DO amalgam restoration placed back in 1989. It seems to have fractured at the disal end, probably within the last three or four days. I have removed the amalgam and now, unfortunately, it looks like you have secondary caries that have invaded the pulp. My guess is that you have a large class II mesio-occlusal cavity in there."

He looked at me in bewilderment.

"What does that mean?"

"It means that I am going to have to give you some root canal therapy."

"A root canal?"

"Yes."

"I don't want a root canal."

"Very few of my patients are eager for them. But sometimes these things are necessary."

"Can't it wait?"

"Absolutely not. But really, there is nothing to worry about. I will administer a nice strong anesthetic, do the work, and you'll be out of here in less than an hour."

When I saw that he was quite unconscious, I took out the two pairs of handcuffs and put one pair on his wrists and the other on his ankles. Then, with a coil of stout rope, I tied him firmly to the chair so that the man was left without the slightest possibility of escape. The truth of the matter was that Ivan had a relatively good set of chops, and there is nothing more sacred to a dentist than a good set of chops. But, even as when in my youth I mentally profaned the image of the mother of God, so now, with years added and my religion changed, I profaned Ivan's mouth. I started with the upper left second premolar, working it out with a pair of pliers, and then moved on, to the upper left second premolar and then yanked out one of the maxillary canines, red syrup running freely from that pitiable hole that had dared to consign itself to my presence.

He started to awaken, gurgling like a baby and lifting the lids of his swollen eyes.

2.

WHAT WILL YOU DO WHEN STRONG ICE
COMES FREEZING EVERY CUNT SO YOU
LIKE TO SEE DRAGONS FIGHTING SO YOU
HAVE TO TRAVEL TO FIND FRIENDS DO YOU
KNOW WHERE I MIGHT AND SO I TIPPED MY
HAT AND HE LOOKED UP THOUGH I COULD
NOT SEE HIS FACE SINCE THE SHADOWS OF
THE TREES WERE EXCEPTIONALLY THICK
I FANCIED HIM TO HAVE AN UGLY BIRDISH
SORT OF VISAGE FROM ITS OBLONG SHAPE
AND THE HORNY PROTUBERANCE WHICH I
WOULD HAVE AS SOON CALCULATED TO BE
A NOSE AS ANYTHING ELSE.

You were a sweet lamb
in the field,
and how you did baa.
You were a sweet lamb
in the field,
friends with the jackdaw.

He replied in a heavy, mountain dialect that was neither Italian nor German, but some rude tongue which hung in between, well peppered with Slavic twists. Myself being familiar to some extent with most of the European languages, I surmised his meaning to be thus:

There is no lodging to be had about here, especially which would suit a gentleman such as yourself. There is, however, a castle a short distance up the way, the property of the Duke of Peralba, whose dominion you are now traveling through. He is known to be hospitable to those of his own rank, often entertaining the lords, ladies and priceless dandies of the neighboring districts. I suggest you move with all expediency in that direction, as the sun is getting low, and the beasts in these woods are far from tame.

Before I could thank the oaf in due form (that is with a few strokes of the flat side of my sword), he hoisted the load of faggots upon his back and made off into the recesses of the forest, as a hare might dart when within reach of the dripping jowls of a famished wolf. I laughed at the peasant's justified diffidence, and without more ado sallied forth in search of the castle, my horse prancing lightly beneath me.

The path gradually led out of the black woods and stretched across a track of desolate ground, whereupon it forked in two: one way narrowing and leading up to a structure of some wealth that was apparent in the distance, the other down into a darkening valley, out of which poked the waving spires of pines. I turned towards the habitation, hopeful of receiving welcome at the door of the Duke, of whose country I was but a stranger in.

The path mounted steeply up a jutting promontory and then proceeded along its rocky face, a sheer wall of damp, dripping stone to one side, an ever-widening chasm the other. The last wink of sunlight fell behind the distant crags and my horse stepped nimbly along the slippery trail, snorting with vigor despite the obvious danger yawning below. As I proceeded, the chilly evening wind nipped at my ears and nose and I was grateful for the lush sable which lined my coat, and thought upon what a blessing it was that such creatures existed, if for no other demonstrable purpose than to warm the skins of their betters.

Turning a bend in the trail, I came in sight of the castle in the near distance, light shining forth from a number of its apertures with an inviting luster. I wasted no time in spurring forward my horse, for the sky was by now decidedly black and the cold was growing more importunate with every passing minute, seeming to insist on its presence being acknowledged by some pusillanimous shivering of my spine or chattering of teeth. The hooves beat crisp along the wet stone, and then hollow as they passed over the wooden draw-bridge. I dismounted and beat upon the great door before me, my heart light with a ready willingness to make fresh friends in that feral land.

It was a number of minutes before I had response, by way of a smaller door, built into the body of the larger, opening but a timid distance, and an immense, hairless lout filling its space and chewing his bottom lip.

"Be quick on your feet, man, and announce my presence to your master," I said, producing a visiting card from my breast and advancing it forth. "Hand him this, my card, and deliver my regards, as well as my express wishes for an audience."

I scarcely know whether the brute understood me or not, for in one single and remarkably ungraceful movement he had the card from my hand and the door shut in my face, me standing, in a most inconvenient position, alone with my horse in the cold. As the situation of the moment did not permit me to rebel against such treatment, I simply fortified myself with a pinkie full of snuff and resolved to make mention of the incident to the master of the house, once I should be admitted into his presence.

As it was, the wait provided me with ample opportunity for admiring the position and construction of the castle: It was placed at the end of the promontory, on an island of jutting rock somewhat set apart and only actually joined by way of the bridge which I had just crossed. One wall of the stronghold was made up of the mammoth points of rock upon which it was built, the others of stones of grand proportion. The battlements reached dizzying heights above; below gaped a gulf of impenetrable darkness. Once the bridge were drawn, it would be as good as impossible for any advancing adversary to penetrate the castle.

3.

You were a green duck
on the pond,
and how you did quack.
You were a green duck
on the pond,
you loved the lilac.

Look at the pansies look at the pansies they were pretty as could be nicer than all coloring combined though not smelling even in the hot morning sun he opened the paper bag and took out a pair of pantyhose tan and very sheer and made him think of sexual intercourse it filled him with a sense of otherness and subtly erotic urgency akin to the brutal.

The express train passed by and he saw the people in a blur—not individually, but as segments of a whole. He adjusted his tie, though instead of straightening it became more disarranged. It was made of silk and was blue. Blue with small dots which were also blue, but of a lighter blue. There were other men wearing ties, and he wondered if they too were conscious of the fact, as of a snake around their necks which strangled them, impeding oxygen supplies to their brains, breaking and collapsing the cartilage and bones of their throats.

CUT TO: EXTERIOR. SAN FRANCISCO, CALIFORNIA. GOLDEN GATE PARK. LONG SHOT OF SAMIR AND STANLEY GETTING OUT OF A CAB.

The camera follows Samir and Stanley as they walk through the park. Johann Joachim Quantz's "Flute Quartet No.2 in E minor" plays on the soundtrack and we see various sights: dogs being walked, people rollerblading, tourists with cameras, young men smoking marijuana, homeless people making love, etc. Samir and Stanley both seem happy; Stanley in particular. They walk past the museums and Stanley admires the statuary. They veer off toward the Japanese Tea Garden. Stanley catches sight of Jae-yong and Azra walking some distance away.

STANLEY: Look, Samir, there's Jae-yong!

SAMIR: Where? I don't see him.

STANLEY [*pointing*]: Over there. He's walking with someone!

LONG-SHOT OF JAE-YONG AND AZRA FROM SAMIR AND STANLEY'S POINT OF VIEW. THEN THE CAMERA CUTS BACK TO SAMIR.

SAMIR: So he is. He's walking with a woman. Come on.

15

[*Samir and Stanley approach Jae-yong and Azra.*]

SAMIR: Jae-yong.

JAE-YONG [*nervously*]: Oh . . . ah—just going for a walk. And you . . . fellows?

STANLEY: We're going for a walk too, Jae-yong. We're walking to the Tea Garden. Will you come?

JAE-YONG: Well, actually we were . . . um . . . [*To Azra*] These are two people that I know: Stanley and Samir.

AZRA [*offering her hand to* SAMIR]: Hello.

SAMIR: Nice to meet you.

[*After shaking Samir's hand Azra stretches out her hand to Stanley. He doesn't seem to comprehend. Suddenly seeming to become aware of her presence, he stares at her body in stupid wonder. He remembers the time he took a manikin and knocked a hole out between her legs and attempted to have sex, cutting himself on the sharp Plexiglas. . . . We hear someone whistling Handel's "Harpsichord Suite in G Minor".*]

4.

approximating some very evil flower-bed my mouth out of which grew many stalks of pain ripe with blooms of pulsating shades of pink and carmine, of luxuriant red and [I] had really only two desires,

1) for it to terminate at whatever cost, and
2) the infliction of deliberate injury on him who was injuring me

a sinking feeling

sand slipping through a net

life flashes summed up before one and [I] could see mine, full of its quiet intellectual endeavors and enjoyments (art, copulation, cooked fish and water) so many images there before me, just like my own photos, those still frozen frames recorded by means of the chemical action of light. Light. But it was her who was foremost, the warm flesh of Leaena, for always had [I] been attracted to large women, liking very much to nestle near their voluminous breasts and bury myself in their folds of fat, seeing Mother naked coming out of the shower, her huge haunches. And love. Love. [I] felt that for her too

a scuttled bark and madly trying to ladle off the fear

hearing was flooded by a thousand thundering sounds, catastrophic, and vision by ten thousand beams of every conceivable hue, as if [I] were witnessing some extravagant series of mirages moving across a completely unknown landscape in one continuous stream of vibrations. [I] felt inconceivable panic but found myself without voice to scream and wondered at that moment in wordless thoughts if all those hot

bushy beard misanthrope a rivulet of whisky drool issuing from the corner of his mouth

a stripe of white expiring in the ashtray degradation and dirtied by shame

streetlight mouth slither gate opened glint of pistol the desire to be fed

you too have a touch of the phantom artiste about you if my heart is drained of all but a few drops of endearment you never know what seeds will produce vigorous plants like clouds shall we say if the platonic liking you have for me is like clouds then we'll have the fair weather of love that is

times with Leaena were really worth this great quantity of suffering. [I] flailed and flung myself through confusions of mud, smoke, sparks and candle flames in succession and then found myself lost in a starless night sky. And each memory, the names of my friends, lovers, parents—even my own name—each of these seemed strange and foreign, as if they were the names of distant countries

and

saw a city of many-storied mansions made of various jewels and surrounded by trees that bore immense fragrant fruits and wonderful nuts in all sorts of odd shapes

women were too thin and [I thought] maybe too frigid and so [I] was soon hurled away by the butchers of evolution and found myself hovering above an island of darkness where the houses were all black and red and everywhere there were black pits, and black roads and the beings that inhabited there were very ugly and very unhappy

caves, ant holes, and grass huts, as if through a fog, charred stumps, black spots, dark ravines, and shadows

lace curtains a painting of a cat, a print of a fish the figure that excites lust, and what better way for a woman to show off her figure than in pants

a pleasant grove and spinning wheels of fire

saw her there with Dr. Valentin on top, him a furiously
working little mechanism. The smell of rotten fruit.
And [I] felt strong longing, strong sexual attraction.
Grunting. There was that split fig spindly branch from
one tree weeping and into it [I] plunged, drowning in a
dazzling and putrid river of molten salt and blood, cur-
dling milk and liquid rubies just sat there on the grass
saying things [I] couldn't quite follow they stretched out
over to me cut away stripping the thing down his teeth
white the vegetables of the trees and shrubs wincing

5.

yes, I am a big woman, a fat woman, and men have to get to accept that if they want to be with me. Victor not only accepts it but loves me for it and it's helpful to hug him against my body and let him know what a good woman is like he buried his seed in me and there were dangers in the birth but in the end the baby came out quite lovely a wiggling little boy

his hair jet-black Jae-yong waits in the living room

watching the streaks the switch branch made in the air and feeling. That's when I realized that his two eyes were set on me. The empty bottle dropped out and it was stinging, but to his ears it must have sounded like I wanted more. I'm hearing through my pain

mattress soft with old semen and fermented vaginal juice

he grabbed Samir from behind, twisted his arm and had him down on the ground. Yves Hermite took the hunting knife out and snipped off Samir's left pinkie.

Samir yelled.

He held onto where his finger had been and his hands were wet with blood.

"I'll go see if I can find you a band-aid or something," Azra said.

6.

flowers blown
when springtime comes
the smoke added palpability to his internal form and,
exhaled, filled the vacuousness of space. At a puff a
minute, it would last him fifty minutes—that is, fifty
puffs, to the two-thirds mark, where all men of good
taste let it expire . . .

"I deemed myself as an eagle among the children of
men, soaring on high, and looking down with pity and
contempt at the groveling creatures below," he quoted.
And then from Beckford: "He cast his eyes below, and
beheld men not larger than pismires; mountains than
shells; and cities, than beehives." Jae-yong yawned and
reached for the glass at his side.

His aunt, Min-jung, played tennis in a private, in-
door court and regularly wrote out checks to a number
of prominent psychoanalysts as well as an East Indian
gentleman whose beard was beginning to gray. She had
a special room set aside for her meditations, decorated
with rare Tibetan thangkas, Japanese prints, an absurd
painting of the god Krishna, and bamboo mats.

The orchestra of sins, if not physically manifest, certainly hung around his person, arguing with his more noble qualities, with all the vehemence of evil having lady on the brain
if you want to play
love is a game of chance
you can never win if you are not willing to risk
his mind said it was right
and his heart
being a flexible and non-contentious organ
easily gave in
feeling a little wickedness was acceptable after all.

The days of material salivation sat in his spectrum as sealed tombs, monuments gathering their first layers of dust. Purée of fowl à la reine, mussels à la marinière, andouilles; these were so many ghosts; good dining was a phantom.

At one point he had subsisted primarily on rillettes of minced goose on toast; at another chicken pastilla, with its rich filo dough, cinnamon flavor and powdered sugar, made up the body of his diet. He had tried out numerous chefs, of both sexes, all nationalities, hoping to find one that would keep his palate amused, in a sustainable fashion. But each one had a few specialities—a few tasty dishes they knew how to prepare—and that was all.

One, a short and demonstrative Frenchman by the name of Anatole, was expert in the art of sauces and stews; he made a superb périguex and a blanquette de veau that was extremely edible. But when it came to making a Malaysian grilled pomfret, a bawal panggang,

the man was helpless. He had not the faintest idea what to do with lemon grass and coconut. Later, a Chinese woman, Pi Lee, was engaged. She had a genuinely broad repertoire: Shanghai-style dumplings of both pork and crab (succulent and spurting hot, flavorful juice like naked wrestlers in the arena expressing sexual force); a pleasant enough jellyfish salad; a bitter melon soup with a very light and meaningful chicken broth.— Really, she cooked quite a spectrum of interesting and savory dishes.—Yet after a month, Jae-yong was frankly bored with it. Though the dishes varied, the hand that made them was always the same. When he was in the mood for a simple pasta carbonara she brought him rice noodles coagulated with ham. For a green salad she served boiled mustard greens doused in rice vinegar a fat Bulgarian gentleman whose flesh white and stiff resembled sweating porcelain an Italian lady of extreme composure with teeth serrated jagged like those of a terrier European gourmands left by the wayside tenderest veal stick of rotten wood in the baccalà a subtle and wormy ephemera a monstrous flavor like that derived from a pat of briny rancid butter
golden troughs
the last Quickstop
wrinkled menus lips moving
characteristic gesticulations of a French waiter
time lapse
a giant lobster sits in front Jae-yong.

7.

Leaena and her son, Stanley, were sleeping in the spare bedroom. Things had been getting pretty rocky with her husband, Victor, so he was staying at their home back in Hermopolis while she visited.

No, I did not see anything. Well, too bad. I think it can be dropped somewhere. I was pretty drunk alcohol. I had been to the village yesterday, we just stayed at home.

"When do you think she is going to leave?" I asked as we lay in bed.

"How should I know," Azra replied. "She'll go when she's ready I guess."

All other eyes were still staring straight into the outline of a dirt road, clearly visible from the end of apathy, the simple courtesy, words jointly meaningless and unnecessary. Not if I wanted a decent nights sleep. Azra was always sensitive. I took hold of her hand and planted a kiss on her tightened up lips.

"Stanley and Leaena are in the next room. Do you want them to hear us?"

I was just trying to tell her how we could be quiet and everything would be alright just some silent humping like two pigs with their mouths sewn shut when the doorbell rang.

I cursed.

"Want me to get it?"

"No. I will."

I got up, put on my pants and a shirt and took my .44 out of the top drawer where I kept it.

"You're going to answer the door with that?" Azra asked.

"Sure."

"Put that stupid thing down and answer the door like a human being," she said, sitting up in bed. "Whoever it is will think you're a maniac. The last time you answered the door like that it was Mrs. Cheng and she still shakes her head about it every time I see her."

"Fine," I said and lay the gun down on the top of the dresser. "Just don't blame me if it's a couple of *real* maniacs."

I went into the living room. The doorbell rang once more and I opened the door. I suppose that I should have looked out the window first, but my mind was on other things.

"My car broke down about a quarter mile up the road," said the man in front of me. "You don't mind if I use your phone, do you? I'll just dial up a tow truck and be on my way."

Aside from the blue nurse's uniform that he wore there was nothing peculiar about him. He had a pleasant, congenial face and very soft eyes.

"You coming from work?" I asked, moving aside so he could enter. "I suppose you're from Thompson's Center. I see their vans driving by on the frontage road pretty often."

"Yes, that's right," he said. "I'm a nurse over there."

The door was still open behind me and I heard what sounded like a snicker coming from outside.

"What was that?" I asked, turning around. "Are you alone or——"

Before I had time to finish the sentence a streak of pain ran through one side of my face. A man, his face taut with bloodthirsty lust, was on top of me, his fists hammering away at the ball of flesh which was my head. Too surprised to struggle, I closed my eyes and accepted the punishment. A voice raged from out of the field of hurt:

"I CAN SEE YOU THINK I KILLED HER BUT I DIDN'T WE HAD A FIGHT USING THREATENING LANGUAGE I'LL TELL YOU ONE THING I WHIP CHAIN MY MALE ART BONDAGE LOOK AT ME WITH NO EXPULSION!"

The oblong and throbbing thought of the next day's newspaper sat in my head, the grainy photo of my own pulverized body beneath sensational headlines ending in an exclamation mark lying motionless in a bath of sweat forgetting for a time I know sometimes shudder through me without electricity amazed at the emotional thrust of my body on the bed is pushed in front of a bright light in my eyes. I was kicked in the side, fixed my arm behind me and the first person I saw when I opened my eyes was Stanley. He was kneeling on the ground in his pajamas. I was hanging from one of the vegas, my feet and hands bound with telephone cord. My head ached violently, and I could feel every heartbeat as a pulse of agony thrusting at my temples. I felt certain that my face was covered with lesions and, by crossing my eyes, could make out the bent tip of my nose.

Azra was across from me, her feet and hands trussed together, like mine, and her arched body suspended in mid-air. Her horror-stricken eyes looked out at me with silent pleading.[1]

I twisted my neck back and saw a man, probably in his mid-forties, kneading the air with his palms. A large scar, with the sutures still fresh, ran across the back of his head, which was bald except for a few scraps of gray stubble. His only clothing was a white patient's robe, tied loosely in the back, so his bare rump protruded. The other man, the one who I had opened the door to, stood before him, holding Leaena, her arms pinned behind her back.

She screamed frantically and agitated her body. The man caressed her fear-tightened face with the red muscle.

Stanley's eyes were shut tight and I could see his lips moving. "He's praying," I thought, and hoped that it

---

1 NOW LOOK HERE MISTER ALL THE EVIDENCE IS AGAINST YOU WERE HEARD FIGHTING SEEN LEAVING THE BUILDING WITH BLOOD ON YOUR HANDS FOUND DEAD IN YOUR APARTMENT THINGS DON'T LOOK GOOD FOR YOU SIGN THE CONFESSION YOU PROBABLY DIDN'T MEAN TO KILL SO MAYBE YOU'LL GET OFF EASY WITH FIFTEEN YEARS.

would do some good. If God would listen to anyone in there it would be Stanley, but I had always had my doubts about God and knew that Stanley was praying because he was scared out of his wits.

I thought about Stanley's father and how he was probably snuggled up in bed watching late night TV back in Hermopolis. I could feel the pain of the cords tight around my ankles and suddenly realized how much I disliked Stanley's father, and, as an unfortunate consequence, Stanley himself. "Don't be hard on the kid," I told myself, even though, from where I was hanging, he had it a lot easier than me.

"Be calm, daughter of Venus," said the Nurse to Leaena, "and don't let Knut frighten you. He simply has a yearning to unveil the secret that lurks behind your Cyprian altar. Let us examine the bud of that dark rose, and know that you will find pleasure in the attacks, and long for sweet death as they become more plentiful."

Leaena began to pant and gasp. Her face became so white that I thought she was going to pass out. The Nurse asked her, politely, to remove her nightgown.

8.

Then the man said to get in there. And when I was in there I could still see through the door and he and the other men were laughing and drinking coffee out of paper cups. Then she saw me looking and closed the door. I could still see the hand lying over the edge of the white tub, one finger slightly extended and immobile. That floor was wet and the water pink and I could hear them laughing.

An oblong block of light came in through the one little window and lit up a patch of the bed and she felt its warmth through the sheet and then opened her eyes and the patch was across the room, against the wall.

She got up, put on her shirt and khaki pants, and went into the kitchen. Amy was still there, her head slumped against her chest, a thin string of drool hanging from her open and decayed mouth. Azra lit the stove beneath the water kettle and began to make coffee.

9.

1. He put a bib around his neck.
2. He handcuffed his wrists and ankles.
3. He tied him to the chair.
4. Woman with spiky green hair sitting on curb in torn nylons.
5. Policewoman naked on violet sheets.
6. Dirty theatres.
7. Erotic dancing and live sex acts.
8. A little packet of dope opened up on the nightstand and a needle sitting full, ready for injection.
9. Revealing her slim, fragile figure to the scorching sun.
10. Mouth open like a braying horse.
11. Glad to service these filthy men.
12. Grab the flabby creatures by the hair, dragging them.
13. The man looked up, letting off a broad, mocking grin.
14. It was Samir.
15. Back into the sluice of narcotization.

16. Reclining on the couch, his body sagging, dripping onto the floor; a pathetic mass of ennui.
17. Little bitch.
18. Stinking grass growing out of their cracks.
19. Stains.

10.

She danced around the room and beat the air with her hands while Knut banged on the coffee table with a candlestick—a stage with no décor sits in obfuscation, no flood lights, bunchlights, spot lights or foot lights to set it off from the rest of the dismal room, the theatre, that solemn chamber that shuts out the rays of the sun like a sepulcher and hides the universe behind its shroud, its curtain. The seats in the gallery are unoccupied, folded up, looking like so many rigged, frowning mouths, and the high ceiling recedes into the gloom.

triangular, bearded face   so sodden   to hell with the mildewy cocks

11.

Samir handed him a cigarette and the lighter and Joe the Sky took the cigarette, broke the filter off, flicked it away and then lit the broken end of the cigarette, the loose tobacco flaring up.

Samir takes the bottle of gin out of the paper bag, unscrews the top and takes a pull, chasing it with the last swallow of Pacifico. He hands the bottle to Joe the Sky who pulls hard and then sets the bottle down between them.

JOE THE SKY: No one understands.

SAMIR: Can't stop abruptly . . .

Samir opened another Pacifico, took a deep drink and then oscillated the remaining liquid in the bottle. The shade of the cottonwood trees was pleasant and on the opposite bank there was an anthill. From where he sat he could see the ants move and, though himself cool, understood the heat of the hill.

And then he saw the bottle, its shimmer and translucence, and how it was raised up one hundred and eighty degrees, its contents disappearing in rapid fluidity down the other man's throat.

12.

Without so much as a word or a whisper, the man led me forward, across a torch-lit courtyard, and signified with a few spasmodic gestures of his hands that if I were to leave my horse outside he would take me into the building's interior. I forthwith secured the reins to a nearby fastening, and proceeded through a thick, black door, amused at the underling's loping gait as he advanced before me. We moved through a number of stately hallways and rooms furnished with antique magnificence, and though they lacked many of the trappings of the times, they nonetheless carried with them the obvious perfume of opulence. There were large paintings of the old German and Flemish masters hanging from the walls, richly embroidered furniture placed properly about, and luxurious Persian rugs which took the chill off the stone floor beneath.

The man ushered me into one chamber, more sumptuously decorated than the rest. A fire was ablaze behind a monstrous grate and candles alight in all the four corners, their glow dancing on the tapestries and lavishly frescoed ceiling. A small, darkly-clad figure rose from one of the seats in the center of the room and moved towards me, with smooth female strides.

"Welcome, Marquis," she said, offering her hand English fashion. "The name of your family is known to me, and I feel fortunate in being able to offer you the hospitality of my husband, the Duke of Peralba. It has been some weeks since we have had the pleasure of entertaining anyone of quality, and I can assure you that he will wish for you to stay as long as possible."

"It is I who am fortunate," I replied, taking her fingers and bowing deeply. "If it was not for your kindness in receiving me, uninvited and unexpected, the cold earth would be my bed tonight and wind my blanket."

I then proceeded to relate to her the circumstances of my passing through that wild country, so far from my own home of Padova—yes Padova, situated along the Bachiglione River, between Verona and Venice, whose recorded history dates back as far as 300 BC, when an invasion was attempted by the Spartans Gauls Hungarians and Venetians a place of great culture and was once home to a number of fine Latin writers including Livy; and Galileo taught at its university, see our artisans at work and browse our wines and cheeses and smell the roasting chestnuts and see the frescoes in the Scrovegni chapel by the founding father of Italian painting and that little masterpiece by Guariento depicting a troop of angels moving through the night sky which hangs in my bedroom back home and the Palazzo della

Ragione and the convent of Santa Giustina which was destroyed by an earthquake in 1172 and later rebuilt by Michelangelo and to all this she listened, displaying all the signs of civilized interest, and I waxed more eloquent, taking note that her austere, petite and pale features gained sparkle with each robust phrase I delivered, as if she were some thirsty plant and I a dashing spring rain.

"Well," she said when I had finished, her lips quivering slightly, "I am sure my husband will be delighted to make your acquaintance. Presently he is occupied with dressing for dinner, an operation which never takes him less than three-quarters of an hour, or else he would have met you himself. If you would be so kind as to follow Miss Vronsky," she rang a bell sitting near at hand, "she will show you to your room, where your belongings have been taken. You can prepare yourself to join us at table, taking what time your own toilette requires.—And have no worries regarding your horse; it is being well tended to by Mullo, the henchman who showed you in—a fellow who, though unforgivably mute, is adept at such mundane tasks."

I thanked her in due form, and followed the woman who had entered at the sound of the bell: a stern-visaged Russian with the impenetrable deportment of a well-trained servant. I was taken to a relatively comfortable chamber whose barred window looked out onto the blackness of space. The ceiling was high and undecorated; a painting hung over the four-post bed of some kind of demonic apparition, apparently female, her loins a ravenous, fanged mouth in the process of devouring a rather startled gentleman. Though I found it an odd sort of image to have hung over a guest's bed, I put it down to the aesthetics of the North, and without lending it further thought proceeded to dress for dinner, unleashing my best pussy-pink cravat for the occasion.

13.

Jae-yong finally got a part in a play during the production of Chekov's *The Seagull*, when midway through rehearsals one of the actors, the fellow who was playing Trepliov, broke his leg and was forced to quit.

"Will you be stop—stopping with us for a while?" mumbled Jae-yong.

Leaena had a nice house, and, as she had a child, she invited Jae-yong over to practice his lines, since it wouldn't do to leave the kid alone. Jae-yong felt humbled by this woman, and could have hardly bragged about being physically or mentally her superior, for she had a magnificent build; huge, she dominated; she was experienced and at first he merely felt somewhat abashed being alone with her, but this was soon supplanted by a secret fondness and being around her he felt his senses heightened, magnified, mismatched, and intertwined, like the poem of Baudelaire's, where he talks about colors and sounds answering each other and describes men as walking through a forest of symbols, for truly he felt her voice, saw her balmy odor like an aura, and seemed to be able to taste her very presence. She mystified him, and all with no effort on her part that workhouse where souls are shoved and sewed up in their proper casings their road bifurcates at the juncture of charisma women become split like a winding trail through a cool forest difficult to find and easy to lose one's way on is what the painters of old tried to capture in their Madonnas and their Ariadnes, her physical beauty not even necessarily surpassing that of her unsuccessful rival often in photographs seeming plain possibly even dull—for photographs can never capture the sublime unless taken by the most expert hands, like those of Ivan who often photographed her naked, and even then they seem to pervert nature, unlike a fine painting, which has a veritable nature of its own, it being wrought stroke by stroke and line by line—a certain air about her that infatuates working on the supple regions of the heart like a trouvère on a lute it dispelled the loneliness that had prevailed upon him and then it did have its sensual satisfaction, for even a bad wine can taste good to a parched throat, seeing this plump driad whose skin caught the light like golden brandy and booze is better than broth and so his reasoning stormed about every evening before going over to her house Jae-yong decided that that would be the night he would declare himself. But the nights passed and words of passion turned into stoic comments and she could see the state of confusion that she threw him into, and this flattered her vanity somewhat and she was alone and when Victor took her in his arms and and and.

14.

When I opened my eyes they were blurred with sweat and tears. I could see the snake-like form of the Nurse moving across the room. A quivering and oozing mass lay prone on the floor. The air was permeated with an unwholesome stench.

"Azra," I murmured. "Azra?"

She was crying.

"Leaena," she whispered. "Poor Leaena."

Knut came in, drinking from a bottle of vermouth, and sat down on the couch. I personally was not a vermouth man, but I knew that Azra was very fond of it. I could see her head turn in his direction and imagined her thoughts.

"She is probably wondering why I am letting that son of a bitch drink her vermouth," I told myself.

The Nurse came in drinking a can of beer.

"Dreaming mortals," he sniveled, striding around the room. "Oh, how much joy I will give you on this evening, throughout these dark hours when the moon is but an elixir of my inflamed juice. This young maiden is satiated, already plummeted to the depths of poetic delight, a treasure buried in her riven chamber, shining like embers of gold. Now, who is next? Who wishes to mount the throne of heaven?"

Through the corner of one eye I could see Knut watching me.

"Him?" the Nurse asked, waving the can of beer in my direction.

Knut lifted the bottle of vermouth to his lips in silence.

"Or would you prefer her?" the Nurse cried, twisting his body around grotesquely and pointing a knuckled finger at Azra.

She let out a sob.

Knut looked up dully from his bottle and slowly rose to his feet, vermouth trickling down his whisker-stubbled chin. He swaggered towards me and stared straight into my eyes. His own were a very pale blue and his eyelids, wrinkled folds of pink flesh, occasionally batted over them. He turned and I could see at close proximity the scar on the back of his head which was suppurating, a yellow puss oozing forth. My gaze dropped to his exposed derrière and I shut my eyes in disgust.

"I'm going to kill him," Knut said, in a clear, calm voice, which I would have never thought him capable of.

The Nurse laughed.

I heard Knut move to the fireplace, his heavy, elephant-like tread filling me with a bilious hate I knew what he was doing sure enough when I opened my eyes and turned my head I saw him coming towards me with the iron poker.

The Nurse pranced towards us, the can of beer splashing merrily in his hand. He smiled at me and then at Knut. A misty look came into his eyes. A thrill shot through me as I saw all the signs of compassion alter his features. Knut's fist grew lax around the handle of the poker. I began to breathe more easily.

"Well, are you going to knock his head in or what!?!" the Nurse suddenly screamed, his face twisting, mouth painted as a hideous oval, white teeth glistening and lips twitching with cruelty.

Knut moaned, his body tensing up. He gripped the poker tightly and turned towards me. His eyes were open wide. He lifted the poker over his head and then naked they were all hauled out on stage fingers pointing laughter everyone was looking.

15.

Something of that childhood disease remained. Invalided.

Jae-yong walked to the house where Stanley was. Sitting on one of the timeworn couches that were prostrating their sagging frames was a diminutive young man with a fresh young beard smoking his pipe pensively and listening to a little hand-held radio that seemed to be delivering much more static than reception. Cesspool of idiots.

Mrs. Cheng opened the door.

He walked down the dark hallway. Stanley liked to paint. As a child he would paint puerile houses and figures, but as he got older and the depersonalization disorder he suffered from became more acute, his limbs seemed to be unresponsive to the idea of forming definite figures with his brush. His strokes often turned into splashes and blobs that he continually refrained from commenting on except for with smirks when asked.

"Say, it's awfully quiet in here. What happened to the guy in the room next-door?"

"He's gone."

"Where did he go?"

"Mrs. Cheng said he left and he's gone."

If he had been a woman his feminine nature might have sprouted forth in gentle waves of bisexuality.

16.

DEMI-GODS MINOR GODS THEOCRITICAL
EXISTENCES VASUS ASURAS APSARASAS CAN
YOU BE HUMAN FOR ONCE SHOVE YOUR
TUSKS WHERE THEY BELONG YOUR HAIR
FLOWING IN ORANGE RAYS THE DISTANCE
BETWEEN YOUR MIDDLE FINGER AND THE
UNIVERSE YOU DEMI-GODS SAYING FUCK SO
COME YOU ELEMENTAL DEITY HANDSOME
IN YOUR TATTERED SAD ORNAMENTED
UNDERWEAR GREASED ELEPHANT SKINS
TOTAL TRASH YOU POSE IN FREEMASON
BLOWJOBS CHURNING THE OCEAN THE
HOLY ONE ANOINTED WITH STRAY BURSTS
OF RED SEMEN THE LITERARY ORGASMS
THAT NEVER CAME THE HASTE SOME USE TO
SAY THEY'RE SOMETHING WHILE BRAMĀS IN
STONE AND BRONZE ARE IGNORED BECAUSE
YOU FOOL CARRYING YOUR CLUB YOU
WORSHIP YOURSELF INSTEAD OF THE GODS
RUBBING YOUR LOINS WITH SANDAL PASTE
DO YOU THINK YOUR BIRTH WAS WITHOUT
BLOOD AND FLOWERED CUNT YOU LIER.

17.

Scene: The Maddox's house, in a small, unidentified town somewhere on the East Coast of the United States. The study of Dr. David Maddox, noted psychiatrist. The study is on the upper story of his home. It is the typical collection of bookshelves, weak prints on the walls, a desk with a phone on it, etc. There is a liquor cabinet. There is a window, outside of which can be seen the leafy branches of a tree. Dr. Maddox sits at his desk, working. He is a man in his mid-forties, with a serious, confident demeanor. He works over some papers, flipping through books and scribbling down notes. The phone rings. He picks it up.

DR. MADDOX: Hello? . . . Hello? . . . Hello, is anyone there!?! . . . Oh, how are you? I thought it was a prank call perhaps. . . . No. . . . Yes, I realize it wasn't. . . . Certainly. . . . Certainly you are, but . . . But you're in distress and. . . . Listen. . . . Listen, Mrs. Biekman. . . . Listen, Mrs. Biekman, I'm fully aware of your condition, but you have to understand . . . Mrs. Biekman . . . Mrs. Biekman . . . Mrs.

Biekman, I am not telling you anything of the sort.
. . . Did I say that? Did I? . . . No, I'm not. . . . I am
not, Mrs. Biekman. . . . I do care, Mrs. Biekman.
. . . I will listen to you, Mrs. Biekman, but . . . but
don't you see that I cannot . . . It's not a matter of
love or hate, Mrs. Biekman. . . . Or life and death.
. . . That's right. . . . No, I am not laughing at you.
. . . No, I do not think it's just a game. Did I say I
thought it was a game? . . . Why, certainly. . . . Yes.
. . . Yes, I do agree with you. . . . That's right. . . .
That's right, you've just got to always keep that in
mind. . . . Well, you've got to tell him so. . . . No.
. . . No, Mrs. Biekman, that's not a valid solution.
. . . No, Mrs. Biekman. . . . We don't use that word,
remember? . . . Well, let me be the judge of that. . . .
Mrs. Biekman. . . . Mrs. Biekman. . . . Could you
just hold on for a minute, I've got a call on the other
line? . . . No, I'm not going to abandon you. . . . I
promise. . . . I'll be right back, Mrs. Biekman. . . .
[*He puts down the phone, gets up and pours himself a
J&B, then returns to the phone.*] Mrs. Biekman. . . .
Yes, Mrs. Biekman, I'm back. . . . No, I was being
perfectly frank with you. . . . Yes. . . . Yes. . . . Mm
hmm. . . . Yes, I completely understand. . . . My
opinion is the same as it's always been. . . . That
was your choice, Ingrid. . . . I don't care if it wasn't
ethical. I too am a human being. . . . I did not force
you. . . . Don't say that, Mrs. Biekman. . . . Don't
say that. . . . Mrs. Biekman. . . . Mrs. Biekman. . . .
Ingrid, listen to me. . . . Ingrid, I am not going to be

emotionally strong-armed. . . . The point is that it's not true. . . . No, I know that wasn't your imagination. . . . . That's not my intention. . . . I never said it was, Ingrid. . . . Listen, you will not. . . . That's right. Because I said so. . . . No. . . . No, I also don't believe that you're capable of it. . . . I am not trying to lead you to disaster. . . . I'm as ethical as I can be. . . . Remember what we talked about. . . . That's selfish, Mrs. Biekman. That's very selfish. . . . That was a mistake. . . . That's right. . . . That's right. . . . That's right. . . . No, that's not what I meant, Ingrid. . . . No, not in the least. . . . Just calm down, dear. . . . On Monday, dear. . . . Yes, you will, Ingrid. . . . Yes, you will. . . . You will still be on Monday. In forty-five minutes you'll be feeling on top of the world. These cases always work out that way. . . . That's right. And I know you don't want to do anything foolish. . . . I said foolish. It means something totally different. We all do foolish things, but that doesn't mean that we're all fools, right?. . . . Of course you're a very smart woman. Anybody who knows you knows that much. . . . I don't doubt it. . . . Anything you want. . . . I promise. . . . Not for a minute. . . . If you have to. . . . Then it's settled? . . . I think so. . . . So I'll see you on Monday then. . . . Perfectly. . . . Yes. . . . Yes. . . . Yes. . . . Goodbye, Mrs. Biekman.

[*He hangs up the telephone and walks to the window with his drink. He looks out dreamily.*]

DR. MADDOX [*to himself*]: Possibly psychoneurotic. Hysterical . . . all about . . . sexual relations . . .

[*There is a knock at the study door. He quickly seats himself back at his desk and starts writing, looking very busy. There is a second knock at the door.*]

DR. MADDOX: Yes, yes, yes; come in, come in.

[*Margaret enters. She is a woman in her early forties who, though handsome, looks worn and aged. To look at her you would think she was older than her husband, though, in fact, she is several years younger.*]

DR. MADDOX [*without looking up*]: And what can I do for you?

MARGARET: Oh yes, dear, just fine.

DR. MADDOX: Well, must it be at this very moment? As you can see I'm quite busy.

MARGARET [*holding up a corner of her dress*]: Well, thank you. It's not new you know; I just haven't worn it in some time. . . . Since that . . . that time. . . . I'm treating today as a sort of a holiday. It's a special day . . . for us . . . for him.

DR. MADDOX [*looking up*]: Then he should be here soon. It will be good to see him. It's been so long. . . . Not too long. Long enough though. Long enough.

MARGARET: And it is such a beautiful day. . . . I was outside and the smell of the apple blossoms brought tears to my eyes. . . . I know it sounds . . . I remember as a girl playing in the apple orchard by our house. Oh, how I adored wandering amongst those blooming old trees! At that time they hardly produced any fruit. . . . But such beautiful blossoms!

DR. MADDOX: I hope he's been burning the midnight oil. Life is, after all, a quest.

MARGARET: And I even picked a branch and put it in a vase of cold water. . . . I put it on the table in the living room. . . . A touch of spring. . . . To brighten things up! . . . [*wringing her hands and looking slightly in despair*] I'm just gushing, aren't I?

DR. MADDOX [*becoming agitated*]: Don't let's bring that up again.

MARGARET: We'll eat roast beef tonight. I know that both you and he like roast beef.

DR. MADDOX: I can't be held responsible for everything that goes wrong.

MARGARET: Followed by a dessert of . . . oh . . . dear . . .

DR. MADDOX: It was something that was beyond my control—beyond anyone's control.

MARGARET: And then we'll sit down for coffee. . . . Or do people do that anymore? . . . Oh, David, I don't want to live in the dark ages anymore!

DR. MADDOX: But he can't be shilly-shallying about. . . . No poetry. . . . No dreams. . . . He must work. . . . Even if the cost is . . . great.

MARGARET: Yes, when I was a girl I saw things that way. . . . I still feel like a girl sometimes. I was a very happy girl you know. You wouldn't think it, but I was. . . . At least that's the way it seems . . . from here.

[*There is a knock at the door. It opens and Rusty appears. The doctor rises on seeing him.*]

MARGARET [*wringing her hands*]: David, it's Rusty! It's Rusty!

RUSTY: I came in . . . but you didn't hear me. I came up. There was talking, so I came up.

DR. MADDOX [*grasping Rusty's hand*]: How are you, Rusty?

RUSTY: Very well, Father.

MARGARET: Look how he's matured!

DR. MADDOX: And how are your studies?

RUSTY: As well as can be expected. . . . And your practice? I assume it's going strongly.

DR. MADDOX: Tolerable. . . . It's doing tolerably well. . . . Patients. . . . Well, maybe; maybe one day you'll know.

RUSTY: I just might.

MARGARET: Oh, he will, he will!

RUSTY: And you, Mother?

MARGARET: You do care about me then . . . a little? Do you hear that, David? He does care. He really cares. It's not like people . . . It's not like they . . .

DR. MADDOX: Nobody says anything, dear. Nothing to do with anything that concerns you, in any case. Sometimes I think if you weren't my wife you'd be my patient. You're always superimposing your own fantastic notions on things.

MARGARET: We can drive to the lake.

DR. MADDOX: The lake! She wants to go to the lake!

RUSTY: Must we talk about this?

DR. MADDOX: Who's talking? And if I were, that's my prerogative. As you know. . . . But you're welcome to . . .

MARGARET: You're hungry I hope? Dinner should be——

DR. MADDOX [*looking at his watch*]: Well, it seems that supper time is not far away. If you'll excuse me, I'm going to go and wash up. You can fill me in about your studies over dinner. It seems your mother has fixed something . . . nice, I believe.

RUSTY: Wonderful.

[*Exit Dr. Maddox. Rusty pours himself a healthy drink and walks over to the window, looking out.*]

RUSTY: The old yard.

MARGARET: You used to like it back there so much. . . . Remember? . . . And you had your friends. . . . I'm sure they would like to see you. . . . Those that are still here.

RUSTY: Do you ever see . . . ?

MARGARET: I really very seldom see anyone. Not after . . .

[*A pause.*]

RUSTY: The old yard.

MARGARET: Yes, the old yard. The old, old yard. . . .
It's not getting any younger, is it?

RUSTY: Not the least bit younger.

MARGARET: But it still is . . .

RUSTY: Calm. Quiet.

MARGARET [*making as if to leave*]: Oh dear. I really
have to check on dinner. I really must. [*She takes
hold of the door handle. Looking at the door she says:*]
. . . It is nice to have you home.

[*Exit Margaret. Rusty sets down his drink on his father's
desk. He looks thoughtfully at the telephone.*]

RUSTY: Nice to be home?

[*He picks up the telephone and dials a number.*]

RUSTY [*over phone*]: Hello. . . . Is that you, Geeta? . . .
Yes, it's Rusty. . . . That's right, Rusty. You sound
surprised. . . . Well, I just got back. . . . Yes. . . . I
suppose so. Not more than usual though. . . . I can't
help it. . . . That's not true. . . . No, I always will.

. . . I don't care. . . . No, not for a moment. It never crossed my mind. . . . I think you exaggerate. . . . What? That would have been ridiculous. . . . But you couldn't possibly understand. How could you understand when is all you do is . . . Yes. . . . Uh huh. . . . Of course you do. . . . It's not a matter of that. . . . Me too. . . . No, there are no tears in my eyes. . . . You don't have to be. . . . I just expect— something! . . . Fine. . . . I understand. . . . I would like to. . . . Yes, I'll be here. . . . Then I will see you. . . . Okay. . . . Goodbye.

[*He hangs up the phone.*]

RUSTY [*to himself*]: Home again. . . . Things. . . . A task. . . . One really has to . . . to finish it. . . . It really must be done. . . .

[*Rusty makes for the door, pauses, and then leaves.*]

[*Exit Rusty.*]

18.

I always liked to feel little Stanley's softness, the softness of that sweet little boy and let him have my nipple, to make him good and strong with my milk. Victor kept telling me that I should not breastfeed him but just do it with the bottle, but a man could never guess at a mother's love and understand the need to make it natural and the union mother and child have to make with their flesh.

There was no more dentist's office for me. I told Victor to find another girl and joked with him that she had better not be too cute.

"Leaena, you're the only woman I'll ever love," he said.

So I got to stay home and take care of Stanley and lay back and dreamed of Ivan, of running my hand through his thick, white hair and kissing his lips. But since Ivan wasn't there I petted little Stanley and kissed him on the forehead.

19.

"They tried to tell me I had been drinking too much."

"I dragged the corpse into her bedroom, and from there into my private bathroom that adjoined."

"I saw how they were naked and I had a pack of Zig-Zags in my pocket."

"My thick flesh hangs like ripening fruit."

"It was lit and I knew that it was all written out."

"My man was like a rutting horse, always ready for a turn in the hay."

"You surprise me."

"He is currently sinking in his own blood."

"Those women looked."

"I took up the great meat cleaver that hung over the counter, returned to the bathroom, grabbing a cutting board which I tucked under her arm on the way. I put down on the toilet seat and then removed all the towels and mats from the bathroom, putting them down in a pile next to my bed. I stripped off my clothes, leaving my body completely naked, a great tumble of flesh, and then went to work."

"The statue was there with the birds on his shoulders, the squirrel at his feet, the top of his head all shaved off and he wore that dress. The sun was up over the tops of the buildings and shining through the trees, coming down on me looking all white."

"My father was a butcher and I often helped at the shop over on Stockton Street, the Sun Sang Market it was called, so I knew how to do it all. First I gave a swift hack just below his jowl, then turned him over and propped his feet up against the back of the tub and turned his throat towards the drain; best to get rid of as much blood as possible so as not to create too big of a mess, since there would be plenty of cleaning up to do as it was."

"I suppose I must now look for a new position—unless of course you choose to poke me with that sword."

"You speak very calmly."

"I have been told that poise was one of my assets."

"I stood there watching as the red liquid slowly seep out of the wound and drift down the drain."

"I was controlled by this dissociative disorder that continually asserted itself, making the trace elements of my psyche take precedence over reasoning and self control."

"My legs wide apart over the body."

"My skin felt like loose painful jelly as I watched my lovers wading in mounds of fetid orgasmic pleasure."

"The meat cleaver was still in my hand, the blade just slightly stained."

"I danced around, waving my arms as I leaped nimbly across the heaps of crawling filth."

"All those women were looking right at me."

"They bathed me in their stinking emissions that stuck to my flesh in thick gluey coats, tangling my body as I gasped and struggled."

20.

He felt the experience and hollowness of it, then saw the light shimmering past his legs and spread across the sidewalk before him.

"You need a ride?" came from the window of the brown Volkswagen Rabbit.

Samir looked at the face of Yves Hermite behind the steering wheel. When he sat down in the car, he could smell the man redolent of some sort of odd cologne.

As they sat down on the couch, a voice, high-pitched and cracked, came from the back of the house:

"Yves, is that you? Is that you out there, Yves?"

"It's just me, Mother," the man called back. "I just brought a friend home to visit."

A withered creature emerged from a darkened hallway. The woman moved precariously, placing her slippered feet with infinite caution. She wore a pink nightgown of a cheap, synthetic material, her arms unsheathed, wrinkled, the flesh hanging loose around the fragile bones.

"You want some milk and pie? I'll fix you boys some milk and pie if you want."

"We're fine, Mother. You can go back to sleep. We'll manage."

The old woman turned and moved slowly back into the dark hallway, feeling along the walls, guiding herself by touch.

21.

I could not, then, gather trying to make light of the situation. And stirred in a corner and saw a flash of diseases uptilted rays of the moon. As he spoke inside, a deer head trophy said a hoarse growl coming and muddy.

"I do not want for the good, but at least they seem to be suitable for us to persuade me."

He did not answer.

By the numbers—everything must be done by the numbers—but the third is the length of a bottle of the evening as we walked according to the sex-abdominal visor, well, to be precise, he heard, as in the highest source of things is quite clear that it was the smell of the deep. And not only by his coming, in the non-orgasmic sense of the word, when already I could see the greater good loves the general effect, but I am seldom caught napping and never caught cutting sheep. I am the one trillion.

"Management of action," I replied.

And he brought me a positive answer so a grunt-banging cigarillo sent a box of sulfur. It was a battery-operated western cowboy gun with light/sound. He fumbled with it for a space of about two minutes. The yellow of the burst, saw a spark from the game. For I have seen only a little while, but the hair is like a feature you can, believe me, compare to a hedgehog. I could hardly understand the dusty areas of my bed, and watch the brilliant flowers after two fiery red ones, watery eyes naturally imbued with a sense of enduring. But he was stronger, which is evidently the wolf he would awake for me, colleagues, let me come in to be moved.

In a sack, to roll on the border of the body of sufficiently small. And I lifted up my voice, for they will hear a horror of hair.

"I think you have sex."

By putting my heart on the horse. The sinew of his thigh, and bowing the knee warmth.

"The elder brother looks up to his own show."

Male muscle fatigue.

"Dig a little rain?"

"Behold, your son, came, and we shall be better soon."

"Last muscle!"

"Abdominal!"

Many hear a gun and go out and rattle.

"I have no feet."

"I will not see my face again in the future."

"Thou sayest well what belongs to another."

"It is wonderful."

"Coagulation of the blood."

22.

*The living room of the Maddox's house, downstairs. There
are two doors, one stage right, one stage left, each leading
to distinct parts of the house. The background is French
windows, outside of which can be seen a yard with trees,
etc. There are several chairs in the room. There is a fireplace
with a mantle on which are various knick-knacks, one of
which is a brass miniature of the Venus de Milo. On a
table is a vase with a small branch of an apple tree, with
blossoms, in it. Margaret is pacing back and forth clasping
and unclasping her hands.*

MARGARET: . . . . And when he comes . . . mere
wishes . . . rare . . . more rare . . .

[*Enter Dr. Maddox from stage right.*]

DR. MADDOX: Rusty down yet?

[*She does not reply.*]

DR. MADDOX: Rusty down yet?

MARGARET: Down and gone I think.

DR. MADDOX: Gone? Gone where?

MARGARET: I don't know. . . . I only thought. . . . For a walk perhaps. . . . Maybe he didn't go. I'm not sure.

DR. MADDOX [*looking gravely at his wife*]: Well . . .

[*Exit Dr. Maddox stage left.*]

MARGARET [*continuing to pace*]: More wished . . . [*She stops, standing quite still*] Well indeed!

[*Geeta appears outside the French windows and knocks. She is a typical young woman of about twenty, neither overly handsome nor ugly. Margaret opens the door.*]

MARGARET: Geeta. How nice to see you.

GEETA: Yes. It's been a while, hasn't it?

MARGARET: I'm afraid so. Too long really. . . . But come in, come in. Rusty's out and about somewhere I think. . . . Though I'm not sure.

GEETA [*entering*]: Well, I can come back later.

MARGARET: Nonsense, sit down. If he's gone, he'll be back soon. I'm sure he was expecting you. . . . Let me check his room. He might be there. Let me check. I'll be right back.

GEETA: Thanks.

[*Exit Margaret stage right. Geeta sits down on a chair. Enter Dr. Maddox stage left.*]

GEETA: Oh, hello . . . Mr. Maddox.

DR. MADDOX: Hello. I'm surprised to find you here.

GEETA: Why surprised?

DR. MADDOX: Yes, why? Things like this are not . . . uncommon.

GEETA: Probably.

DR. MADDOX: And you . . . look well.

GEETA: Thank you. I've been running in the mornings.

DR. MADDOX: In the mornings?

GEETA: Yes, in the mornings.

[*A pause.*]

GEETA: And doing other things also.

DR. MADDOX: Other things.

GEETA: . . . . Why, yes.

[*Margaret enters stage right. Dr. Maddox sees her and looks perplexed.*]

DR. MADDOX [*to Geeta*]: You'll excuse me, won't you?

GEETA: Of course.

[*Dr. Maddox exits stage left, looking over his shoulder at his wife somewhat maliciously as he leaves.*]

MARGARET: Well, I've found him. He was upstairs. He said he would be down in a minute. I put out some coffee and things in the dining room for you two. . . . I thought maybe you'd like that.

[*Joe the Sky appears behind the French windows, unnoticed by both Geeta and Margaret.*]

GEETA: Do you want me to wait in the dining room?

MARGARET: Only if you want to.

GEETA: Well . . . it seems like it might be best.

MARGARET: Yes, go ahead. Rusty should be with you in a few moments.

[*Exit Geeta stage right. Margaret paces back and forth clasping and unclasping her hands. Joe the Sky can be seen peering in the window.*]

MARGARET: . . . . Oh, how strange, how strange. . . . And do they realize . . . do they even realize?

[*Joe the Sky knocks on the French windows. Margaret opens one.*]

MARGARET: Hello, can I help you?

JOE THE SKY: I don't know, but I need it. I really need it. My name is Joe the Sky. [*Taking off his hat.*]

MARGARET [*timidly*]: Nice to meet you. My name is, um . . . Margaret.

JOE THE SKY: The pleasure is mine, Margaret. Because I like you. [*Entering*] Not afraid of me, are you?

MARGARET: No, I don't think so. I try to understand people.

JOE THE SKY: I bet you do, Margaret. I bet you do understand me. Can you believe I was once a little boy, Margaret? But I was. I really was.

MARGARET: I'm sure you were a charming child, Mr. Sky.

JOE THE SKY: Joe the Sky, Margaret. Just call me Joe the Sky. Over the willow weeds, Joe the Sky. . . . I was once walking down the street. . . In Albuquerque, New Mexico . . . in 1987. And the light came to me. . . . Do you believe me, Margaret?

MARGARET: Yes, I believe you, Joe.

JOE THE SKY: Joe the Sky, ma'am.

MARGARET: Joe the Sky.

JOE THE SKY: Joe the Sky.

MARGARET: Tell me, Mr. . . . Joe the Sky . . . are you, I mean . . . you must be lost. . . .

JOE THE SKY: Margaret, I've been lost for a long time. [*singing*] That hat by the side of the highway . . . is a hat without a head. . . . That hat by the side of the highway . . . sits on sand dry and dead. . . .

MARGARET [*clasping her hands to her chest*]: You have a beautiful voice, Mr. Sky. I love song and dance. We get so little of it around here. As a girl I would dance. . . . Dance like the wind. . . . But, well . . . Well, now everything's different.

JOE THE SKY: Margaret, someday you and I will dance together. Would you like that? Would you let Joe the Sky dance with you?

MARGARET: Well . . . someday. Someday maybe when I have the strength. I've been so tired lately. . . . So tired.

JOE THE SKY: You're a shining star, Margaret.

MARGARET: Thank you, Mr. Sky. . . . Thank you very much. It's kind of you. . . . to say so.

JOE THE SKY: Tell me, Margaret, I don't mean to be rude or anything, but you wouldn't by any chance have a little liquor around the house, would you? . . . Just a couple fingers worth . . . for a sinner.

MARGARET: No, Mr. Sky. No, I wouldn't have anything like that around the house . . . for a sinner. . . . But . . . but for you I think I might.

JOE THE SKY: Thank you, Margaret. Thank you ever so much.

MARGARET: Wait here. [*Exits stage right.*]

[*Joe the Sky looks around the room admiring things. Dr. Maddox enters from stage left, observing him from a distance without being noticed by Joe. Joe takes up the miniature of the Venus de Milo from the mantle and puts it in his pocket.*]

DR. MADDOX [*coming forward*]: Excuse me, sir! May I help you? What are you doing in my house? What is it you've put in your pocket? Who let you in? [*Grabbing Joe's arm*] Show me what you've got!

JOE THE SKY: Hey, lay off me, man. I don't have anything.

DR. MADDOX: Dammit! Who let you in here?

JOE THE SKY: Margaret did, man; just lay off.

[*Margaret enters carrying a bottle of J&B and a glass.*]

MARGARET: What's going on here, David? Why are you holding that man's arm?

DR. MADDOX: He's a thief. I caught him stealing something. How could you let a person like this into my home? What's that you have in your hand? Liquor! Is that what things are coming to around here?

JOE THE SKY: Lay off Margaret.

DR. MADDOX: Margaret? How long have you known her?

MARGARET: Leave the man alone, David.

DR. MADDOX: What's he got in his pocket?

JOE THE SKY: Who says I got anything in my pocket?

DR. MADDOX: Give it to me, give me what you took!

[*They struggle. Joe ends up striking the Doctor on the jaw.*]

DR. MADDOX [*falling back*]: Damn you! Damn you. Call the police, Margaret! Call the police!

MARGARET [*running to her husband and kneeling beside him*]: Oh, David!

DR. MADDOX [*to Joe the Sky*]: You're going to pay for this. Do you hear me? You're going to pay for this.

[*Joe runs out, exiting through the French doors.*]

MARGARET: Oh, David! He didn't take anything. I'm sure of it. What is there to take?

DR. MADDOX: My jaw. [*Rising*] I'm calling the police. We can't have people like this haunting the neighborhood.

[*Exit Dr. Maddox, followed by Margaret, stage left. There is a pause. Enter Geeta followed by Rusty from stage right.*]

RUSTY: . . . so there wasn't much I could do.

GEETA: Not much you were willing to do, you mean.

RUSTY: It's not that I wasn't willing, but it wouldn't have helped to go digging things up again.

[*A pause.*]

RUSTY: Don't you think?

GEETA: Think what?

RUSTY: That I was right.

GEETA: I can't tell you.

RUSTY: But you have an opinion?

GEETA: You know I do.

[*A pause.*]

RUSTY: So you're indifferent?

[*A pause.*]

RUSTY: So you're indifferent?

GEETA: No.

RUSTY: But . . . ?

GEETA: It's hard to explain. . . . It scares me.

RUSTY: What are you getting at?

GEETA: I'm not sure. . . . I don't know. . . . Maybe if I knew, or could explain, it would be . . . you'd find out it was something you didn't want to hear.

RUSTY: You . . .

GEETA: I surprise myself too.

[*A pause, after which Margaret enters hastily from stage left, looking distraught.*]

MARGARET [*to Rusty*]: Oh, there you are! Your father's been beaten.

RUSTY: Beaten?

MARGARET: No, he was punched!

[*Exit all stage left. A few moments later Rusty returns.*]

RUSTY: It's all ridiculous. Just a game. A silly, frivolous game.

[*Enter Geeta.*]

GEETA: He's asking for you.

[*Exeunt.*]

23.

"Don't you think he is getting to be too old to be breastfed, Leaena?"

"Victor," I replied, "he's only three years old. He's just a little boy."

"I don't like the way he looks at you when you open up your shirt."

It was obvious that he was jealous of Stanley. He had no right to try and come between me and my boy. It is true that I was not giving Victor as much sugar as a husband should probably get, but frankly I was sick of laying on my back bored stiff while he crawled around on top. I wanted to be twisted and turned into all sorts of shapes.

I liked to feel Stanley against my body slow and nether the kind of suffocation he enjoyed his own mountain of flesh teeth and muscles baby's hands were very small and almost translucent.

his wife lay there exhausted loins like a split fig a mushroom is glossy and pure before the maggots come he beat her up his clothes sheltering the white meat of his body then he said something under his breath about the breastfeeding and I left, slamming the door after me. I drove to the grocery store and bought some soda and donuts and a chicken to cook for dinner, then went and had a hamburger before returning home.

24.

Yves Hermite took another puff of the joint, set it down in the ashtray and, taking up his pen, continued where he had left off:

> Stanley pointed the gun at Knut. The Nurse lunged forward and Stanley wheeled back towards him, pulling the trigger. The shot resounded throughout the room. The Nurse reeled back, letting out a hideous shriek, like a whipped donkey. The can of beer flew in the air, a tail of liquid following it. Knut dropped the poker and jumped on Stanley.
>
> The Nurse was bleeding but not dead. It looked like he had been shot in the shoulder. Knut had wrestled Stanley to the ground with ease and sat astride him. The blue patient's robe had come undone. His almost bald head was glistening, the fresh scar standing out red against the sutures.

The Nurse raised himself on one elbow. "He shot me, Knut. He shot me."

"GOT TOO MUCH SPICE ON THE TOILET ALL NIGHT," Knut yelled in response.

It was all up for Stanley. I closed my eyes again. I did not want to see anymore.

CUT TO: INTERIOR. LECTURE HALL AT THE UNIVERSITY OF HANOVER, GERMANY.
Dr. Maddox stands at the podium in the darkened lecture hall. Behind him is projected a complex diagram which includes a number of striking images, such as a grown man being breastfed, a galloping horse with a naked woman on its back, etc.

DR. MADDOX: But I am inclined to believe that the phallus is pulled by strings, for there is little other explanation for its virile nature, and the emotional attachment engendered is certainly not unlike that which a child feels for a favorite toy or puppet.... And it is said that in ancient times, they would slaughter it at the doorstep, as a sacrifice, and the women would sing and dance with joy at the event, thus ushering in a new stage of human intellectual development. . . . And so the research data gathered . . .

25.

The screw of the need to learn by Yeon Jae-yong decadent and went to Rome, in order that the truth about
the bosom, and wine, and slow (not that it is written in
it), or the sick of the palsy pomatia snail of Burgundy,
the radiator back to white-haired villainous robbery to
as it increases the problem. He was not interested in
Gros-Gris or dipped in dark clothing when most hor-
rible. This snail grows up to commercial houses and
pride that looks fake fat balls into the television screen,
but who are no more than a Van Gough painting on
a coffee mug. Trident prepared a plate of escargots a
la bourguignon, just slightly, and put his fingers into
a dove, and the dream of all the scales, but that it is
easy to cultivate as the Gros-Gris. September slash pine
forest near Brive in the derrière like a fat peach. He
has prepared a special series of ecological space flights.
And to attack them. Beautiful black snails in prison
by the court. And they watched with great interest the
strange feeling of their kindred, slithered in the wet to
his servants over the mire of the hermaphroditic state.

By May he had two thousand five hundred delightful little Burgundies, each one as delicate as a dewdrop

and as precious as a jewel. These he put in a ten square meter greenhouse, within which grew rows of young lettuce, chicory and basil interspersed with finger bowls of an excellent 1956 Cliquot. As the snails matured he pulled out the best: those whose shells were of the largest diameter and possessed the most distinct and uniform coloring. These virgin mollusks he set aside in individual boxes, to hibernate until the next season. Those which remained he harvested as they matured, sinking them in boiled rose water for 3.5 minutes and then removing the bodies from the shell. The hepatopancreas of these snails were particularly delicious, so he let them remain, transferring the whole bodies into chilled water which had been previously dosed with sea salt. Kneaded together with butter, garlic, pepper, shallots and parsley, then returned to the sluiced shells, his effort produced many a good meal.

The following spring he took his breeders, the finest of the previous year's crop, and set them in pairs amongst little beds of daffodils. He smiled as he saw the snails approach each other, extend their liquidy antennae and coquettishly touch, often drawing back with sudden, shy impulses. They would meet upon a slender stalk, dip and crone their shiny little heads and then, together, seemingly arm in arm, circle the flower's corolla and disappear beneath the nearest petal.

All of the snails were gorgeous, but two were particularly remarkable. The color of their shells were perfectly uniform and their size was incredible: one had a shell diameter of 74 mm, the other of an astounding 80 mm. He named them Adam and Eve.

26.

INTERIOR. POLICE STATION. DAY.
We see Jae-yong sitting in the questioning room at the Police Station. Lieutenant Burke sits opposite him. Another plain-clothes officer, Dan, stands against the wall smoking a cigarette.

JAE-YONG [*desperately*]: But I didn't do it! I didn't kill her, and I don't know who the hell did.

BURKE: And New York?

JAE-YONG: Yeah, the girl in New York . . . I admit it, but I didn't kill Azra. Don't look at me like that!

BURKE: You were digging her up . . .

JAE-YONG: But I didn't do it. I didn't kill her.

DAN [*rolling up his sleeves like he's going to get rough*]: I guess I better show you what matters.

CUT TO: EXTERIOR. THE NEW MEXICO FOOTHILLS.

Azra has been looking at Jae-yong. He is dressed neat and his hair is clean and shiny. She looks at him and Jae-yong cannot help but notice her body; to notice and evaluate every female anatomy he ran up against, indistinctly imagining what it would be like to caress them.

CUT TO: JAPAN. NIGHT.

We see shimmering spikes of emerald grass and ravines of precious gems. The black air is moist and bubbling with pearly eggs let loose from the wombs of terrestrial beings. Fungal trees sprout with slippery sticky pelts. Drunken twigs scroll the ground. Boundless fragrances fill the air— rose, clove, eau de cologne, the ocean, sulfur, sawdust, paint thinner, green horse manure. A number of women are lying on a bed of cherry blossom petals. They are naked.

WOMAN #1: . . . tongue moistened fingertips . . .

WOMAN #2: . . . the finches have disappeared . . .

WOMAN #3: . . . the fetid odor of love that streams through the air . . .

27.

CUT TO: UNIVERSITY OF URBINO. DAY.
The audience is all women. Most of them wear eyeglasses. Some chew on pencils or take notes while Ivo Bogliolo, professor of graphology, is speaking, pointing to a large projected image of a letter penned by Yves Hermite.

PROFESSOR BOGLIOLO: . . . As can be seen, the vertical and horizontal expansion of the handwriting is pronounced, even to the point of showiness. This is said to be a sign of the need to exhibit oneself, the need to be admired. The middle zone of his writing (*a*, *n*, *o*, *w*, etc.) is monotonously regular, which is said to be the mark of a regimented individual, while the upper zone (*f*, *t*, *l*, etc.), or the sphere of the spirit and mind, is full of high floating *i* dots and confused *t* crossbars, indicating the instinct for superimposing phantasy on reality. The lower zone (*f*, *g*, *p*, *y*, etc.), or the sphere of biological demands, is full of triangular loops, betraying self-consciousness and repression. The slant of the whole hand is definitely leftward, marking a defiant nature. . . . Lastly, a comment on the signature. To begin with, the capital letter is overemphasized, which is generally believed to be a compensation for deficient self-esteem. But a strange contrast of points here develops, for the name is also underlined, which is said to betoken ego emphasis. The last bit of interest stems from the final appendage, for here Signor Hermite lets off with a slash, a protrusion zagging off the final *e*, that looks not unlike a sort of sword or bayonet. This kind of final motion is said to denote aggression and it's interesting to note that Napoleon Bonaparte had this same sort of mark at the end of his signature. . . .

28.

He had his little Rothkos and a little Kandinsky; he had a tiny drawing by Paul Klee and a sculpture that looked like an Uecker; bad watercolors by unheard of Bauhaus artists and a number of other odds and ends he had picked up on his travels: a mask from New Guinea, a painting of a featureless head from Russia, some Swiss paraphernalia and a few Native American knick-knacks. By far the best thing in his house was a set of two rather bizarre photographs taken by a friend of his who had passed away in odd circumstances.

"You like those, do you?"

"I should say so."

"The artist, Ivan Borisov, is no longer with us."

"Such talent!"

Sunny kissed Yves and then the two men wandered into the living room and sat down on the couch.

Sunny took up a loaded hypodermic needle and handed it to Yves.

"You first," he said.

"What is it?"

"Just a little something I got from a friend of mine—a prominent member of the American College of Neuropsychopharmacology."

"Your friends are all . . . interesting, it seems."

"I think so."

a little prick

no got mine got

for devimetric standard

subsliding into the reveling smothered in criers in the region of purge having the remarkable tendency to undulate at the slightest environmental fluctuation hair was of the color of kumquats brushed strait in the style of the ancient Egyptians as any connoisseur of blue blood can tell you hips fastened in a pair of transparent dungarees genitals breathing rapidly and the feet of this creature were sentenced to spend the evening in a pair of maroon pumps which he kept cutting off

he watched as great lads ate their fill of good pink protein jangling like young birds in spring their hair glistening with good oil

making small golden stacks

udders sagging with sweet milk teeth hard kissing his scraggly chin hare lips growing paying little attention to his submissive voice and just became more active something like snot running down their faces in the colder part of the room they had each other's quiet love little stars bleaching the sky with bits of hope

walking through the people with his bundle, slinking thoughtfully through that wandering sea of meat. Arriving at his building he opened the door at the ground floor and climbed the beaten-up staircase. He lived on

the third floor and had to wind his way past all the other apartment doors on his way up. He found something unsettling about all those closed doors staring him in the face every day. Since he had moved in he had hardly seen any of his neighbors, just one couple that lived across the hall from him who always seemed a little scared
wild horses à la Visigoth
that doesn't sound very attractive
playing tricks upon travelers
drawing a herring across the trail

29.

we see no farce stumbling comedy, emotional drama or tragedy, no pantomime or masque

his mind always seemed to teeter between the sublime feelings of love and those ancient ringings of savage hate that instinctively gripped him sending the everlasting urge for animal satisfaction, the lurking necessity for lady flesh; the crude base longing to display his anthropoid vigor

you've become so subjugated by the rôles you play that you're like a ghost. You're always acting, one can never tell if what you say is a line from a part you once played or just the lees of your drained heart

her hips full and arms plump like a veritable Titian lips had something playful about them, like they were always about to let out a laugh. Her skin was supple and moist, with a fine down on it, the filaments a dozen times more inconspicuous than those found on the stalk of the poppy or petunia—a comparison which is doubly applicable since she herself seemed more fit for a hot house long humid days in a motionless atmosphere than to be subjected to the vagaries of the world at large with its changing seasons, rain followed by hail followed by snow, which, after beating down the delicate plant, buries with its contours smooth and refined gentle as mink and as firm and white as the tissue of the cassava root—a tuber whose milky insides are permeated with minute purple veins, just like the pale bodies of certain women.

and lying twisted on the thick flower-patterned quilt. Samir drove the needle deep into his vein

love is a fickle thing, and unless it's lodged in the breast of firm devotion it always flies about.

30.

He shifts the gardener, making him plant and plant those obsolete vegetables, those purple hyacinth beans, once favored by Thomas Jefferson, which matured into bleeding red pods containing cyanogenic glucosides, poison; young and prehensile, the pods of devil's claw resembled okra; long and thin kipfelkrumpl potatoes, skirret, the ornamental yet exquisitely edible Joseph's coat. Then winnigstädt cabbage, which twisted into a lovely pointed head and, turned into sauerkraut, went well alongside a few roast squab. The blue shackamaxon bean made a black polenta, sapid, reminiscent of a creek at night; served with a shank of lamb, anointed with pinoli and claret gravy it was ideal for supping on during a mellow spring night.

These early, almost aboriginal vegetables, he found tasted best along odd sorts of game—rich meats. The classical horsetooth amaranth went well with roast civet. Evening primrose added a certain piquancy to a Brunswick stew cooked with gray squirrel. Opossum and Malabar spinach. Baked crane with barely cooked crosnes and syrup of violets. Bear and Texas bird pepper. Beaver tail and cymling squash. Woodchuck with welsh onions. The combinations were numerous; but not infinite.

Item: Three green geese in a dish, sorrel sauce
Item: Potage of sand Eeles and Lamprons
Item: Galandine for a crane or a Hearne or any other Foule that is black meat
Item: Lamb's ears with shallots
Item: Chauldron for a Swan

He was delighted with a recipe for stewed larks:

> *First takes them, cleans cleanly them, cuts away their expenses, then places in good wine a tray, puts out good rice polishings, places in the liquor, places in the hot-pot, they have cooked a while there, then takes some currants, washes cleanly them, admits in the soup, with a sugar, cinnamon, with several plank bread, admits the lark, lets them eat together, then casts off six dozen roses, places in a tray, then to have in the tray of consomme, eats for them.*

The recipe "To still a cock for a weak body" he found infinitely amusing:

> *With a not too old red cockerel, kills him, death, hugs him above, breaks out him in*

*a bone them breaks. Then takes root fennel,
naturally, mature, the violet leaf and borage,
place the cockerel, puts the anise seed, rubs
the licorice, therefore fills the dormitory of
your dick, places one-fourth rosewater, one
bottle of white wines, 2-3 dates. If you have
golden-yellow wine, it will be better, receives
one centimeter plum, covers it, blocks it with
the pasta, places in it the water that a pot
seethes with excitement, burnt 12 stoves under the hot pot, in the pot has been putting
12 cups. When it soaks these many cabinets,
then takes out, opens it, admits in the bouil-
lon a pot, sooner or later will give the weak
person it.*

In his search for new peculiarities, ever inclined
to the tender, he bent his brow toward the smaller
creatures. In Australia he tried fried witchety grubs,
enjoying, in a morbid sort of way, the creamy texture
of the inside as it contrasted with the crisp and delicate
skin. Venezuela offered the roasted tarantula, which he
imbibed daily throughout his three-week stay—six to
a plate; he cracked them open like crabs and, with naked fingers, advanced the bits of delicate flesh between
his parted lips. . . . While touring China he sampled
scorpion soup, and then, with the stingers removed,
the same creatures *crudo*. . . . The mopane worms of
Botswana he ate while sitting on an old log, under the
flaring sun, the only civilized man for a hundred miles
round. . . . In Mexico, ant larvae and pupae called esca-

mole, as well as fried red agave worms. . . . Mealworms. Stinkbugs. Creatures that crept under rocks, existed in roiling bundles of multiplexed consciousness, honeycombs of living, crawling matter to be sampled in his nomadic journey through culinary dissipation.

Yet, as interesting as bugs were, they were hardly worthy of being more than a passing fad;—insects, though varying in flavor and possessing more finesse than cows or sheep, he found to be rather limiting as a culinary experience.

Shih Hu, the ancient Hun ruler, would, for special occasions, have one of his wives beheaded, roasted and served to his guests, while the uncooked head was placed on a golden platter, and displayed, so that all could admire her beauty while they supped. A far cry from the debased form of cannibalism practiced by those of the Donner party, on that snowy California pass over one hundred years ago.

Yes, Yeon Jae-yong knew full well that the eating of one's own kind was in disrepute, but he tended to the belief that it was something of a modern prejudice. After all, many a stately being had tasted the flesh of human. Richard the Lionhearted was said to have enjoyed curried head of Saracen, prepared with "saffron of good color." Abaga, the great-grandson of Genghis Khan, often partook of his enemies, boiled and minced with chives. Amongst the Tartars, human flesh was consumed with surprising regularity, the breast meat of young girls, reportedly of exquisite tenderness, being set aside for the repast of nobles. Countess Zahra de Báthory disposed of a total of six hundred virgins, both drinking and bathing in their blood in order to keep herself young. Louis XI, during his great illness, drank the blood of children as a tonic.

Of course, that most unusual of tastes could hardly be said to be reserved for the aristocracy. While the Aztec king Samirzuma dieted on the still-beating hearts of his enemies, his people grew fat on their flesh, boiled and served with squash blossoms. The Raft of the Medusa, the subject of Géricault's monumental painting, which resides in the Louvre, was a craft on which the famished ate each other. Maupassant, in one of his tales, spoke of French soldiers slaughtering and eating their most exhausted companions while on the march, without food, through the deserts of the Middle East. Jeremiah Johnson ate over two hundred livers of Crow Indians. Herodotus tells of the Padaeans, who fed on their own sick and aged. In Egypt, during the dawn of the thirteenth century, endophagy was rampant; boiled babies and roast youngsters became a part of everyday fare.

The Maori of New Zealand are now told to enjoy the hogget imported by the invaders and, under no circumstances, to indulge in the excesses of their ancestors. . . . The practice of men dining upon men seems to have been reduced to cases of mere necessity, such as in the episode of the plane crash of the 1972 Uruguayan rugby team, the surviving members, upon being rescued, stating that they had formed quite a taste for rancid brain and lung.

If the sensible man is considered one who adapts himself to the customs of the time and place in which he lives, then Yeon Jae-yong could by no means be qualified as a sensible man. But the narrow lanes, crowded, filled with the bleating of the common drove, were not those by which he traveled. He preferred to go off the beaten path. In his view, the habits of society as a whole had been long decanted from the decorated glass vessels of old, into plastic, present-day jugs—far more utilitarian, able to be handled by clumsy and plebeian hands, but altogether lacking in taste, refinement and the subtle aura of opulence. If the current grouping of humanity expected him to play by its rules, it was mistaken. As far as Jae-yong was concerned, the game was still his.

His inquiries led him to the Amazon of Brazil: The Huasca tribe, who dwelled along an offshoot of the Rio Tapauá, still, according to report, cooked every eighty-fifth inhabitant on the sixth full moon of the year. At that time, so went their tradition, the eating of human flesh was especially propitious. It rejuvenated the tribe for the coming seasons.

He lost no time in making his way to Lábrea, where he hired an Indian guide to escort him on the more troublesome part of his journey. They went up the river in a canoe. During the night, an insect laid its eggs in his cheek, making it swell to the redness and roundness of an apple. He caught a spell of fever. The mosquitoes bit in abundance. He sipped gin and tonic from a canteen and stared into the green masses of undergrowth around him: branches wreathed with vines and snakes, the sponge-like forest floor crawling with tens of millions of insects. Birds of all sorts hollered from the canopy above. Occasionally he caught sight of a monkey or sloth. Fish, tucuxi and manatees swam by the boat.

When he finally arrived at the village, a dirty patch of ground nestled amongst the dark forest, his body felt like a single raw wound, an aching pillar of flesh. . . . If his estimations were correct, the local feast would soon be commencing, as he had managed to arrive on the very day of that hallowed event. . . . He had the guide inquire for him. . . . The head villager, naked and serious, with coal-black hair clipped as with the guidance of a bowl, nodded his head. . . . He invited Jae-yong to join him in the repast, which was then boiling. . . . Jae-yong ate his supper as the sun set and the sounds of the wild jungle filled the air. . . . A woman with thin, pendulous breasts handed him a large leaf on which sat a kind of stewed flesh . . . He sampled. . . . It was savory. . . . The villagers eyed him with great concern as he imbibed the strands of meat, and sucked on the gristle before him. . . . He was offered a white liquid to drink. . . . The flames of the fire danced, the liquor took effect, his stomach became unsettled and things swayed
with moon so bright
under you he loitered
scrounged
with eyes blinking
beneath that
which was mouth
and a ghost
began to sing
about blood
a thousand years old and the next morning found him in a hut of mud and straw, a family of Huascans piled up around him.

31.

INTERIOR. LECTURE HALL AT PRINCETON
UNIVERSITY. DAY.
*Dr. David Maddox sits at a table alone on the stage.
Behind him is a bank of blackboards covered with child-
ish, erotic pictograms. Around three hundred attendees sit
in hushed silence before him.*

DR. MADDOX [*into a microphone*]: . . . the striking
similarity between the act of Jacob, when he poured
oil over the stone, and the lingam worship which we
have been discussing . . . the holed stones of Carlow,
surely only served a single purpose . . .

CUT TO: RUMPS AND HIPS.
*His body transforms itself into a golden vulva
sun mast
and we see men having sex with wedding rings
rocks
clefts and lozenges.*

The cross is raised higher
sending flowering shoots
deep delicious
she sold her plasma
by the quart. Her hands and legs trembled, though vice
would sometimes abate the spasms. Stomach, rump,
hips and thighs. She was a hypochondriac, a minor
kleptomaniac. She feared the weather, insects, heights,
frogs, balloons, the future, believed in bad omens,
avoided anything with the number thirteen.

She walked the streets, pressing her lips willingly
against whatever surface came her way. She dreamed
of her child as she sat on the curb. An ambulance
screamed by. The sun was setting. Night. Encouraged
perversions, paranoia, hysteria.

After he used the toilet he came out, but she was not
sitting there anymore and Jae-yong was in the yard with
the motor running and a joint jutting from his pursed
lips. They moved through unfamiliar streets, which
were very quiet, then past a waste treatment plant that
smelled very evil, and the joint was passed to Samir.

There was shackled darkness behind the hills and a
kind of captivity that gripped him from within, and,
even though he could not take hold of it, it went with
him.

Wild sunflowers grew along the side of the road, as
well as bunches of knotweed and cows came in from
the sparsely vegetated flats and ate. The men drove past
a sill of extrusive, black rock, which a small creek ran
below. Russian olives grew thick around the water and
the damp soil was marked and disturbed by hoof prints
where the cows had come to drink.

When Samir had begun to sense where he was, he directed Jae-yong off the county road and into the bubbling hills. There were no road signs, and as Samir called out directions the roads became more and more rutted and hostile. They passed no cars and there were no houses, just that untainted bleakness.

Azra sat on the chopping block.

There was silence. Jae-yong took out his cigarettes and lit one.

"How is everyone doing?" asked Amy as she walked up.

She looked like an old woman. She was only forty but looked like an old woman and her face was gaunt and hair stringy and steel-colored. Both she and Azra wore army fatigues.

Amy looked like an old woman. The sleeves of her jacket were rolled up and Jae-yong could see the scabs on her arms. He could see the imprints of the dead veins like lines in wood where termites had burrowed. Her eyes were set deep in her skull, on her collapsed face. They were neither profound nor mysterious, just deep and dead looking.

Her mouth opened wide and red as she talked. Several of her teeth were missing, making it like a gash; naked flesh, corrupt and inimical.

Azra got up from the chopping block and went inside. She came back out with a honeydew melon. Giancarlo took it from her, cut it open with his pocket-knife, and handed everyone a slice. They ate the melon and spit out the seeds that Giancarlo had missed scraping away with his knife.

"This is some good melon," said Samir.

He ate the melon and felt it cold and wet slide down into his empty stomach. The innermost part of the melon was cream colored and very sweet. Going toward the rind it was a lime green and not as sweet but the flesh was meatier and more substantial.

Jae-yong did not eat his slice of melon. He held it between his fingers, but did not eat it. He watched Azra eat hers. She looked at him but her face was without especial content. Seeing her wet mouth close around the flesh of the melon stirred something inside him.

Amy threw her melon rind off into the weeds and proceeded to roll a cigarette.

Jae-yong looked at her arms and understood what it was.

"Will you bring it?" Amy asked. "God knows I need it."

32.

Dearest Mother!

I cried last night.

You are the only one who really knows me, and I still blush when you call me sweet. Yes, you have a son, and I dreamed last night that I searched throughout your drawers for it. I could not find it, and awoke in tears.

Do not blame Uncle Alain. After all, am I not here for you to take care of? For me, you are irreplaceable, and the dumplings that you cook are more than just a meal. They are a simple fare, but a food of security and wellbeing.

Do you not notice, on holidays, when it is just the two of us, how happy I am? You have often suggested that I should invite a guest, but some things are best left private, and the candles we burn on those special occasions do wonders to your skin.

If you knew that I had let another woman call me son, would you be upset? I fear so, and dare not tell you of my habits.

What kind of a flower would you be if you could choose? I have always imagined you as a white orchid, with your stem long and slender, and your petals opening up with golden pollen.

I myself am a rose. My red color does much to attract, but also repels. I cannot help it that when I am picked I prick, but for you I will always exude perfume and dew.—Yes, all these years it has been me who has absconded with your special soaps—the avocado, myrrh, jasmine, and those shaped like plums and other fruits. It has been an ongoing joke, because you must have known where they went, along with your stockings.

But you have been a lenient and good, Mother. Your little boy will not leave you for the others despite any rumors you might have heard of the opposite. If I were a brave man I would pluck out my moist and beating heart and sacrifice it, adorned with silver, at the altar of the matriarch.—See, it is true what you have always said, about my romantic notions.

33.

"I want the gray one," said Yekta.

Zahra in the meantime had made friends with a lighter colored pup. "I don't want that one, I want this one," she said.

Yekta named her dog Jae-yong.

"What are you going to name your dog?" Yekta asked her sister.

"Samir."

"They certainly are cute," everyone said about the two puppies.

Zahra and Yekta played with them like they were also children.

Along the fields, Jae-yong snapped at bees. Samir, excited by youth, would chase his own tail. When a chariot went by, they would run after it.

At the Festival of Mithra, Zahra and Yekta tied bows in their hair and ribbons around the necks of their pets. Mani, the town alcoholic, fed Samir and Jae-yong strips of grilled lamb, saying, as he ate one himself, "It's very good material."

The following spring the family packed up the wagon. Shafaat said that she could not stand another season in that place. Her brother, Alain, had been living in Thinis for a number of years. Pressure was put on Sunny to move the family, so he did.

"I hate to leave where I grew up," he said; "but I'll do it for you, Shafaat."

A place was made for the dogs in the back of the wagon. The family pulled off onto the road and headed west. They went past Baba Riz in the rain and spent the night in a Danikash motel. The next morning they visited the holy sights for an hour before continuing on their journey. The dogs were taken for a walk and were more than happy to get out of the wagon.

"Samir can't stand being shut up in that wagon," Zahra said.

They made their way through Mesopotamia, then cut across a piece of Jordan into Israel, down to Jerusalem. The sun was just setting when they got out of Jerusalem and the desert looked ominous in the low light. Chariots and huge wagons pulled by twelve-horse teams sped past them. There seemed to be an endless line of vehicles, forming a train that receded into the distance of the hills. Jae-yong sat peacefully in the rear of the wagon, but Samir was restless and chased his tail around and around.

"When are we going to stop, Father?" asked Yekta.

"If we keep going we can make it to Pelusium tonight," he replied.

"The children are tired, Sunny. We need to stop," said Shafaat.

They continued on a couple of more hours and then stopped for the night at a motel outside of Rhinocorura.

"I'm going to let Samir walk around a little bit," said Zahra opening up the back of the wagon.

Samir jumped out and ran around wagging his tongue and tail. The motel they were at was right by the road and chariots commanded by young shirtless men were continually whizzing by. Samir ran out and barked at the chariots. Zahra called to him but he was so excited that he did not seem to hear. He started chasing the chariots and one hit him and knocked him into the middle of the road. Zahra screamed. At the risk of getting hit himself, Sunny ran onto the road and picked up the body.

They wrapped it in a blanket and put it in the back of the wagon. Early the next morning Sunny went into a field in back of the motel and dug a hole with a shovel he borrowed from the motel manager. The girls and their mother came out and they buried Samir out there in the poor soil of Rhinocorura.

34.

I cannot wait, but do, and walk through these narrow rooms, float, like a helium-filled balloon, an object of such lightness. But—then there is the weight of my heart. My hands clench, for they too are emotions, women, or the hands of woman, white, smooth yet full of anguish, love, the need to tear that comes. From these ignoble associations, these hollow dreams that imprint upon me the lash marks of his desire, the disintegration of his tongue—don't laugh—for I long for no more than a kiss. . . . Oh, liar, yes, that's me; because I do, and long for, demand, more than physical quenching, but times, days, years of sovereign feeling. . . . Without hurt, without the painful minutes, seconds that pierce as needles—for now, now these hours gouge.

Should I just stand here and moan like an animal bereft of all sensibility? A cow, a goat, a hippopotamus damp with jungle waters? Am I not her, her of the long legs, of the plump vagina; her who thinks, makes him red and breathe, labor? Yes, I am a leaf that is still green and will blow, quiver high in the boughs and blow. . . . Yet alone, waiting, me, the other . . .

My world is a cube.

Is it ice?

Do I gamble?

For, though I am a leaf, I must go, walk the lanes with my chin upright, my lips stiffened up, flanks proud, life ahead of me, an infinite spray of gold, a river of lilac running to a tear-dampened grave. . . . For cry over me they will, he must, will you?

So slowly I rinse my face, away with the sorrowful reflection—take up my purse. Yes, I open the door with caution, look at the telephone with longing, tainted with displeasure, akin to grief. . . . And then, abruptly step out, slamming the door, decision. A little pride and self-respect.—Let us not sink too far.

That I don't become hysterical, is amazing to me—I can appear as though all were a pool of warm milk inside. . . . The man, he is that, who smiles, must admire, my breasts, of ambrosia, of life, my cheeks of subdued longing. . . . Is he not a traitor, to his, yes, yes, yes—the woman curled up on his couch; and the dog he walks? . . . So typical. That's what we say, you know, because they, they are so typical of themselves.

He nods—a gallant—stoop with their thoughts, selfish, cowardly, without regard for me, us, our true feelings, the truth of our core.—But let me be flattered—bow to me, bow to this temple of pain. . . . Oh, a snowflake that melts at the slightest touch, a gentle thing that vibrates, it syncopates.

35.

a head propped
sharp steel
weight;
and imbecility
swinging legs
skin clean and good
testes are Herculae
dripping with ancient passion
wrestlers and boxers
wearing garlands of mint
and doused in oil of civet—
they eat honeycombs
while stretching their limbs
and dream
of having sex
in the circus
a boy in an uplifted toga shouts out
for strong wine
as he stands on one leg
and emits a jet
of phosphorescent urine

a thing more rare
than milk of birds
soft bosom alive
bison chalked by some primitive hand
where the hell and why this sex this place one which I
never really wished
to enter
chinless disaster dropped him on his head
and afterward always
those garden gates
creaking
those weeds
those dim lights
kissing garbage lips
the same tendencies
inculcated with a savage riding crop wet leather lush
hide naked shoulders dream of the *Madame Moitessier*
of Ingres large-thighed women of Rubens the *Dama di
Elche*

Myrna stout but attractive not particularly talkative
but eyes that whispered she had blazing red hair the
extremely pale skin of a heliophobe.

36.

Finally Azra and Stanley came wandering out and he was
happy to see her give him a friendly smile which wiped
away the lingering fear that he had been as he and Azra
were on tour and Stanley followed Azra around always
walking behind her in deferential awe his head bent
and eyes glassed over reflecting her body within and she
treated him like an infant talking to him in a caressing
tone and smiling at his simple-mindedness and outside
waiting for their cab they looked out over the ramparts
at the city below a misty film embracing its catacombic
opulence and seagulls soaring overhead on the alert to
scavenge what they could and they felt the impression
of ablution bestowed by the clear sky up above with its
broken blueness casting the cool light of late afternoon
over the gazing threesome and Azra was taking a late
bath happy to submerge her body in the warm water
and hearing the buzzer she hopped out of the tub and
going to the intercom pressed the button to release the
door downstairs calling over it that the door was open
and she thought it must have been Jae-yong and hearing a rustling at the door she called out and imagine

her embarrassment when Stanley came wandering in standing at the open door and she was quite nude her little feet arched over the edge of the bathtub and her breasts peeping out over the froth of the bubbles that her white body was immersed the body's form becoming vaguely visible through the breaks in the foam and the veil of the water.

37.

Sunny started work for a chain hardware store. The family lived in Hermopolis. Shafaat's brother lived in Thinis, which was much more countrified, but there was no work around there. Shafaat herself got work at a condom packaging plant so that they could have enough money to survive. Every morning she put on her blue polyester uniform with her name sewn on the breast and tied her hair up in a nylon scarf.

They lived in a little two-room hut in a bad neighborhood.

"We just cannot afford to move into a house right now," Sunny said. "Hopefully after a year we can get ourselves a place."

There was no room for pets, and even if there had been it would have been likely that someone in the neighborhood would have eaten Jae-yong, because people were so hungry.

"You can keep her out at my place until you get a house with a yard," said Uncle Alain.

His house in Thinis was on a hill surrounded by acres and acres of country. They brought Jae-yong out there and the girls were sorry to leave him.

"We have to get a house soon so that we can get him back," Zahra said.

At first they went twice a moon over to Thinis. They would have lunch with Uncle Alain beneath his date palms. Afterwards, the girls would run around the fields with Jae-yong.

Eventually, however, they started appearing less frequently. An occasional visit was missed, then many moons went by without them showing themselves. The truth was that the family was settling down in Hermopolis. Zahra and Yekta were attending domestic cult lessons and had friends who they wanted to spend their time with. Sunny, upon moving into the city, had thought it would drive him crazy. He had said that there were too many houses and chariots for him to have any peace of mind. But in the end he adapted the best. Leaving town became a real burden for him. He really did not want to spend his time going back and forth to Thinis.

After several years Sunny and Shafaat managed to purchase a house of their own: a palm-lined street where all the houses were more or less the same.

"Now that you have a back-yard to call your own I suppose you'll be wanting Jae-yong back?" Uncle Alain said to Sunny.

"Sure, sure," Sunny replied absently.

The truth was that he had more or less forgotten about the dog. The girls certainly never brought the subject up and he had been inclined to think that Alain would keep her forever. He did not address the problem directly and, eventually, Alain began to get pushy.

He said that Jae-yong was not his responsibility and if Sunny and Shafaat did not come and get him he would himself bring the dog to Hermopolis.

Finally Sunny was compelled to go to Thinis to fetch Jae-yong.

In the time Jae-yong had been living with Alain he had had his left front leg broken twice while chasing after chariots. As he aged the leg turned horribly arthritic causing him to limp and move slowly like an old person with a cane.

"Come on, boy," said Sunny, summoning him into the back of his new four-horse chariot. At heart he felt sorry for him. He remembered his brother Samir and how he had dug a hole early one morning outside of Rhinocorura and buried him.

Jae-yong arrived at the house in Hermopolis happy. He wagged his tail, opened his eyes wide and licked Zahra and Yekta's hands.

"See, he knows who we are," said Zahra.

Sunny could not help thinking that the dog had a better memory than his girls.

A prefabricated doghouse was purchased from where Sunny worked and put in the backyard. Aside from feeding time no one paid Jae-yong much attention. He grew lonely in the little back-yard. There was a world out there, but he was not a part of it. His big brown eyes grew sad. The food put before him he would not eat and his hair became matted. Zahra one day tried to brush him but he snapped at the young woman and bared his teeth.

"He's getting so I don't know what to do with him," Sunny said.

Jae-yong became more and more isolated in the back-yard. Around his kennel no grass grew. He rolled in the dirt. Shafaat complained that the dog was making her yard unsightly. She was embarrassed to have the neighbors see it she said. Sunny appeased his wife by telling her that he did not imagine Jae-yong would be with them much longer.

"I hope not," Shafaat said.

One day Jae-yong dug his way out of the yard. He burrowed under the fence and squeezed his body through.

Whimpering, he went down the road, limping on his bad leg. Something was calling him away. . . .

38.

He pondered the notion of human coitus zoological quadrupedal method places between the hills and water and now mounted looking into each other's eyes as they exhaled their ecstasy, often assuming the trembling pose of affectionate and tender devotion plant life prickly pear cactus ripe with their red fruit.
pocketknife was in his hand. He began to violate the hole and laughed to himself
infertile
stiff with aggression the movement was perceived by his eyes
against the very blue sky on which clouds floated.
the nomadic impulses of ancestors
the male approaching from behind
     Lucretius, in his *Ars Amotoria*, strongly recommended a posteriori reversion the inevitable question of intercourse per anum, a method said to have been most preferred amongst the Spartans, and one Aeschylus even referred to as the pure honor of the a a ah ahhhh ah a a sexual aberration? People curled together like worms in a can, little caring for decorum.—Considering

the built-in limitations of the human frame, citizens seemed to practice a remarkably diverse array of a a ah ahhhh ah a a Aretino, in his *Sonnetti Lussuriosi*, told of twenty-six methods, each one delightfully illustrated by Raphael's pupil Giulio Romano. The *Puttana Errante* of Veniero described thirty-two positions, while *The Perfumed Garden* mentioned forty. Gedün Chöpel, in his Tibetan text translated as *Treatise on Passion*, elaborated on sixty-four arts of love.

The very fact that nearly every man and woman he saw lurking along the sidewalks or shopping in the stores for sustenance, regardless of attributes, had a secret life in the bedroom was a weird tale indeed. Animals performed the function quite out in the open, while humans seemed to find it necessary to mask the act, either through shame, or a sense of propriety which they dubbed civilization. Better by far to have it as it was in the ancient days, when going to the gymnasia or the race courses, the young men could be seen wrestling naked with the maidens, who were also naked.

Yes, the Greeks of old were quite open in their mention of amatory pleasures. Jae-yong recalled the words of Herodorus, describing how Hercules devirginized all fifty of the daughters of Thestias in a single week. Such feats of eros were of great interest. Jae-yong himself had known a woman who would gaudens in quattuor tempora in noctem; and a friend of his, not long married, had informed him that after being separated from his wife for ten days, culmen pervenit sexus viginti sex horae spatium, dum ipse in bis. For men, to have twelve orgasms in a day is considered a feat, and it is known that more than fourteen is extremely unusual. Olivier, Charlemagne's knight, reportedly had sex with the daughter of the Emperor of Constantinople thirty times in a single evening, which was far short of the hundred he had bragged capable of.

"Those kind of stories are absurd," Samir had once remarked when they were speaking on the subject.

"Look," Jae-yong replied, smiling quietly, "tales of bedroom acrobatics are like fishing stories: one always needs to divide the size and quantity by four. If someone tells you they have caught a twelve-inch trout, you can be sure it is only three at the outside."

Gedün Chöpel strongly recommended the man to concentrate on bringing "joy and passionate arousal" to the woman, and went on to elucidate the arts of making erotic noises, slapping, biting, pinching and role reversal. He spoke of the signs of a woman's interest, such as shaking, flesh vibrating, secretionem feminam, flushed face, frozen eyes and quae in superiore parte organi ortu vuluae. And certain suggestions, such as mordens et inferius labrum manu mentum superioribus auribus uberum suctu et frictione in alis et faucibus, seemed to Jae-yong as good a way as any of going about the business.

It was indeed interesting to note how the peoples of the Indian Subcontinent concentrated their attentions often enough on placere mulier dum consuetudinem in Occidente semper satisfactio curari. The Book of Genesis mentioned coitus interruptus, masculum organo quod est dictamen recedente prius, as a form of birth control. Certainly the woman who is born to witness this act cannot be overly happy, herself having been excited without the consummation of detumescence. Indeed, there was no question that, as far as the female was concerned, the method of coitus reservatus was strongly preferred. It has even been said that a woman only reaches a genuine peak textbook case of the perfect male intercourse a short while by the tide of amours when opium was applied to the glans junkies shooting up finding beauty in flaws thrills of romance laughed and joked psycho-sexual constitution through mud pits the skink advised by Plinius Secundus, sparrow's brains advised by Aristotle, lambs testicles advised by Cartolomeo Scappi, simple goose kidneys, as advised by Martial, to be sufficiently efficacious, easier to obtain, than bone marrow of leopard epicurean instincts had led him on the hunt of the flesh, always on the lookout for piquant and unusual.

A smile crossed his lips as he recalled Delphilia, undoubtedly one of the prizes in his collection of lusts. He had met her in New York, while riding the number six train. . . . She sat down next to him, as small as a child, a squint to her eyes and a lameness to one foot; yet a face, jointly oval and petite, which was full of unusual contours and lively expression. As luck would have it, she opened her mouth, a delicate organ filled with two rows of fine, pearl-like teeth, and asked Jae-yong which stop Grand Central Station was—she was staying nearby, at the Hyatt. . . . He lost no time in engaging her in conversation, and quickly won her trust with his refined manners. . . . They got off the train at Grand Central and he walked her to the hotel.

Dinner. Champagne. Flirtatious conversation. Her room. Delphilia undressed and stood before him like a doll. In the course of the evening the woman revealed herself to be the most wild and diverse of lovers. She was a compact and oscillating ball of concupiscence, which, through seemingly spontaneous combustion, burst into flames;—brilliant flambeaux which licked at and stoked his ardor.

39.

The figure walked along the silent and empty street, slapping the traffic meters as it went. Abruptly, he ducked in between two buildings, one large, taking up the better portion of the block, the other a small outbuilding. He saw the light blue of the security guard's shirt stretched taut over the fat belly. The man, in his ungraceful uniform, went leisurely down the hall, his heels clicking, then turned off, and disappeared around a corner. Samir moved toward the other building. A small window, just above head level, was cracked open. He slid it over as far as it would go, hoisted himself up and squeezed through the opening. Inside, his feet rested on an office desk, which was just below the window. The room was cross-hatched with various depths of shadow and transformed, from its daytime existence, into a forlorn and vaguely mysterious place.

He climbed down to the floor, accidentally knocking over a framed photo of a woman with red hair—though he only realized she had red hair a few moments later, when he turned on the desk lamp, so he could see better.

He tried prying the candy and chips machine open, but without success. He tipped it to one side and wobbled it around, then kicked it.

He made his way back to the desk, and opened one of the drawers. Inside were a few pens and pencils, some odd papers, and a copy of *Men's Fiesta* magazine. He flipped through it. On page fourteen there was a story, with a by-line of one Yves Hermite.

He began to read, becoming vaguely excited as he did so:

The contemporary party is little more than a dreary affair. To stand in a crowded room eating a cracker mounted by a slice of ham or sliver of cheese, exchanging banalities with ludicrous women who have the tendency to neigh rather than laugh. Those countless introductions to people who have little more in common with one than air mutually breathed (a mixture of vicarious perfumes, cigarette smoke, and the fumes of middle-grade wine). All these accoutrements, gaudily pinned upon the social occasion, do little to intrigue, and a great deal to repulse.

The Cloudmans' party was in no way an exception. They had invited me and I went. I knew that they needed a certain quantity of artists with which to adorn their establishment; lend it the air of an intellectual soirée. I am generous: I sacrificed an evening of independent existence to the monotony of their entertainment.

As I stood lost in the crowd, a plate of hors-d'oeuvres, which had been forced upon me, perched on the fingers of one hand, a vessel of new wine in the other, I sighted a face of fair and engaging countenance. The owner, a woman of not more than twenty-five years, sat alone on a divan, the space next to her perfectly suited to my rather athletic figure. I advanced.

"Do you mind if I sit here?" I asked.

"Not at all," she replied. "I was getting lonely all by myself."

"But you are in a crowd."

"Yes. Alone in a crowd. What could be worse!"

"Especially for one with such beautiful eyes."

She did not blush. I set down my plate of deviled eggs and smoked whitefish on one side, hooked one leg over the next, and continued to converse with her.

Her face was round and of an extremely pale complexion. Her hair was of a chestnut shade and luxuriant. She dressed with extreme taste. I began to forgive the Cloudmans their invitation. I did not mind dedicating a little time to the creature next to me.

As we talked I made a rather amusing comment regarding the establishment's décor. The young lady laughed, and, in a sort of spasm or mirth, jerked her arm back. Two canes, which had been leaning against the divan, came clattering to the floor. I got up, replaced them, and sat down again.

"It seems that the arm of the divan has become a depository for people's canes," I said.

"They are mine," she replied. "Both of them."

"Oh, I am sorry," I remarked, rather embarrassed, and realizing of a sudden that her legs had, indeed, not so much as tapped since our acquaintance commenced.

"Don't apologize," she said. "Aside from the legs I am in perfect health and certainly don't want to be pitied. Two years ago I would have been walking around the room."

"I see," I said, taking note of the amorous curves of her body, and glancing with interest below.

"I can tell that you are curious," she smiled. "You might be shocked by the story; but I don't mind telling it."

Even though I knew it was a breach of good manners, I let her continue.

"I had an abnormally happy childhood," she said. "So I suppose that is something I will always be grateful for. At the age of thirteen, however, both of my parents passed away while traveling in South America. My aunt, on my father's side, Aunt Eliza, took responsibility for my upbringing. I had never really liked her, but, at first, I was grateful that at least I had a place to go. I never saw her smile. Two big black hairs grew out of the tip of one of her eyebrows, by her temple.

"Unfortunately, the woman was not only unkind, but extremely parsimonious—when it came to me that is. For herself she would buy all sorts of treats and goodies. Chocolates, silk underwear and nice clothes. But for me it seemed she could hardly spare a dollar. . . . I was made to dress like a boy, in the cheapest kind of slacks and T-shirts. I know it sounds petty now, all this materialism, but at the time is made me quite miserable.

"As I grew a little older my physical body became quite lovely. At the age of fifteen my figure was as full as Aunt Eliza's. When we walked together men's eyes were inevitably drawn to my own person, even though I was dressed wretchedly, while my aunt was dressed in very ladylike and somewhat audacious attire. I wished it was otherwise; because she punished me, emotionally, for a beauty I had no control over. Don't smile, a pretty girl or woman knows very well that she is; it is not necessarily vanity.

"In any case; one day Aunt Eliza bought herself a pair of especially nice blue pumps, of Italian design. It was not as if she needed them; she had dozens of pairs of shoes. I myself only had one pair of old sneakers. I begged her to buy me a pair of pumps, similar to her new ones—I begged her until tears came to my eyes; but she flatly refused and became very angry.

"I suppose I should have been grateful to Aunt Eliza for providing me with shelter and nourishment, but I was not. I felt abused, and what is worse, totally unloved.

"One day I snuck into her bedroom while she was out back inspecting the flower garden. The pair of blue pumps were there, near her closet door. I really could not help myself. I tore off my old sneakers and thrust my young feet into those beautiful and elegant shoes, the things which, at that moment, symbolized for me both the coldness in my aunt's heart, and all the joy in the world that I had been denied. I traipsed around the room, swinging my hips; looked at myself in the mirror, posing. Of course that is just when she came in. I had not heard her. She moved as silently as a snake. I froze, my mouth wide open. She advanced; threw me to the floor; tore the pumps from my feet and began to beat me with one.

"It was only a short while after that that I found myself at an all-girls boarding school in New Jersey. I suppose Aunt Eliza thought she was doing me some kind of disservice by sending me off. The truth, of course, was that nothing could have made me happier. In all honesty, I have hated only one person in my life, and it was her.

"To be on my own was wonderful. My natural spirit, my inner confidence, came out. I took part in the school activities, and became popular, with friends to talk to—people who said genuinely nice things to me!

"Suddenly time began to pass so quickly; and, before I knew it, I was at Princeton University, on a scholarship that I had earned myself!

"Boys, men, were very attracted to me, and I wanted so much to be loved and desired. It sounds naïve, I know, but I truly enjoyed teasing males, without ever having the slightest thought of giving them what they so ardently desired, for all my true companions were of my own sex, and we all understood how to make each other happy.

"A little over two years into university life, that is, a little over two years ago, I heard that Aunt Eliza had died. She was found in her home by the cleaning woman. Apparently she had overdosed on Xanax. Strangely enough, the news depressed me. She had left no will. I was her closest living relative. The inheritance was surely not large, but I was not about to turn it down. She had made me suffer; her money and property were some compensation, after all.

"I returned to the house in which I had spent such wretched times. It all came back to me as I made my way up the walk and inserted the key in that old, familiar door. For some reason I was surprised on stepping in: the place was neat, and had a nice, clean odor about it. I suppose I had expected it to smell of putrefaction; to see her body lying there, a mousse of worms and filth. But nothing of the sort. It was just an old house in which an unhappy woman had died the week before.

"I walked around the lower floor, inspecting the gimcracks and wondering how much the house and all its furnishing would bring. I ascended the stairs and looked in my old bedroom. It had been redecorated; it looked nothing like it did when I had slept there. I smiled to myself; rather sourly I imagine. Her room was down the hall. I went in. It was the same as it had always been. I could almost feel her negative vibes permeating the place.

"I opened her drawers, inhaled the aroma of sluttish celibacy, found things I shouldn't have found. I looked out the window, at the yard below. I thought I heard something and turned. They were sitting right there, near the closet door. I picked them up; weighed them in my hands. It was a natural instinct to take off my own shoes, which were now very stylish, and put on the blue pumps which had fascinated my pubescent mind. They did not go on easily. They must have been a size too small. I walked around the room, feeling them grip and pinch my feet. I stood in front of the mirror; a beautiful young woman wearing ridiculous footwear. The color was atrocious . . . much too bright . . . the style passé. . . .

"Disgusted with myself, I sat down on the bed in order to yank the shoes off. I pulled, but they would not budge. I tried to wiggle my feet out, but the pumps seemed to grip tighter. In frustration I slammed a foot against the floor, and cried out in pain. They were strangling my poor little toes!

"I tried to pry one off, putting the heel against the sideboard of the bed, and then, quite upset, collapsed on the floor and wept. I sat there for a long time, scratching at my ankles and feeling sorry for myself. Finally, I got up and stumbled downstairs. My feet were swollen, and I could not walk well. I found oil in the kitchen and poured it over the pumps, thinking it would loosen them, but it did nothing of the kind.

"I was exhausted and angry. I ate a few crackers I found in the cupboard and then climbed upstairs and slept in my old room; slept with those awful blue pumps still glued to my feet.

"That night I had a terrible dream. Aunt Eliza was there, screaming at me, but I could not make out what she was saying. She shook her finger at me while screaming those words which seemed to have some kind of deep and sadistic meaning. It was as if I had affronted her in some irreparable way and she was scolding me and telling me that punishment would be forthcoming. My knees were being beaten with a mallet, then they took me and hung me by my feet from the branch of a tree. I couldn't see their faces. They were below me, pulling my hair."

40.

TURN THE COUCH SO ITS FRONT IS AGAINST
THE WALL BUT CAN'T SIT SO PUT ITS BACK
ON THE FLOOR DARKNESS NEAR HIS BODY
VIOLENT LOVE KENNEL THE CHILD'S DOOR
WAS OPEN SHE WAS NOT THIN THE SOUND
OF A TRUCK ENGINE EGGS FRYING IN A PAN.

"Why do I do it?" she thought as she dropped a
handful of small pork sausages in the hot pan. They
replied, sizzling, and the smell, as it sometimes did,
brought forth an epiphany of nostalgia.

Cooked food lay on the table.

He began to speak, apparently in harmony with
the proteins ingested. Hearing his words, she nodded,
smiled. In a way, it was a relief that he talked, then
teased the child. She loved him. She hated him. A slight
warmth was felt by Servilia between her hip bones.

"When he wants to be nice he's lovely," she thought.
Then she wiped the child's mouth.

A vague act of comradeship.

The terror of the early morning was removed by the
appearance of a misted, bright orb hovering low over

the swamp, which she called a lake. The kitchen table was scattered with the traces of an eating.

She found herself naked under the warm fluid of the showerhead.

By the time she put the child in the car seat she was completely dry. Pulling on to the road she nearly hit a man out walking. For a moment she wished that she had, then she saw him wave and the bald crown of his head and his age and she waved back.

"If all men could be like that," she thought. "Friendly even to strangers."

The sight of the raw meats filled her with a certain pleasure. They were the dead meat of once living things, in the plastic wrapping without any obvious relation to life. Music, filtered through discreet speakers, soothed her and brought out certain primitive, pseudo-emotional instincts in her being. The smile of the cashier made her feel that she was an integral part of the community.

Later that day, the man who was jointly her husband's best friend and her lover came over. During sexual intercourse she tried very hard to enjoy herself and even cried out. Afterward, thunder growled outside and lightning cracked and she saw the rain fall past her window.

He ate and looked at her, occasionally raising his eyebrows as if hoping thereby to communicate. The house sat under tall pine trees and even though the sun had come out and birds sang the unlit kitchen was full of shadow.

A piece of cold sausage lay in the pan on the stove. She grabbed it, then rammed it into her mouth.

Gunshots could be heard from across the swamp where sportsmen shot ducks.

When he came in she saw by the expression on his face that he was upset.

She tried to explain.

"I love you," he told her.

Closing her eyes, she tried to blot out the sound of his voice. She thought of a gurgling brook, a woodpecker, the white sands of a beach, a wicker basket full of shellfish.

She stood motionless. Moths beat against the porch light, fragile and tragic. Walking out, into the darkness, she felt the moist grass beneath her bare feet. She gasped for breath, stuck out her tongue. Her husband's head appeared in the living room window, pressed against it, looking out. Clouds swept past the bright moon. Asleep, she accidentally drank dish soap instead of coffee.

41.

sweating stone
blindfold
head propped
weight
imbecility
legs
lilacs are blooming
they stand
catching
the last
of the evening light
whipped around
all day
by the wind
tonight
they will feel
spring cold.

42.

The playground is shiny black, wet, the oblivion of asphalt. Puddles—full of long worms which the children pull dangling out, throw at each other; stomp on their liquid forms and laugh.

Stanley's thin, bloodless body swims in baggy clothes, feet slop in wet shoes and drag him across the playground, schoolbell ricocheting through to his tympanic membrane, causing permanent buzzing and partial deafness in old age, when his jowl would drop and cheeks hang limp and baggy.

Yves Hermite ushers them in with a thin smile of gravity, eyes surveying his young disciples, running noses, ratty hair—a mob of tender shoots; grub in the mud. He says little things that stir students' spirits, straightens ridiculous comedy tie, a limp cravat.

Stanley's mind still stung and mother's plum-red face and strawberry-in-cream eyes still pendulated before his consciousness blasphemy on her hot tongue the sound of kisses sang through the air and now he would sit very carefully he would sit thinking of large nipples.

The old orthography business on the chalkboard hands raised in the air answers squeaked out fine blue eyes and tragic-lined Germanic haircut sat there across from Stanley chewing pencil sat there he lived in a run-down house by the tracks and his mother reportedly slept with other women and then when the milk spilled off the counter in the morning Leaena probably kissed him told him she loved him and went back to bed giant and naked blue eyes glistening in his run-down house by the tracks a sea of milk white on the floor but Yves Hermite was now smiling haunches pressed against his desk, copy of *Where The Red Fern Grows* efficiently grasped in a prim and bony hand. Filthy manes swaying in stale still air, pencils charting new territories in binders, notebooks, over blue-lined paper. The voice of Yves Hermite strides out, emotional, powerful, image-invoking (a touch of a lisp); hounds and hunts and sorrows of pets and boyhood and early fire-arm experimentation . . .

The ceiling was dragons, wicked things, skeletons with axes, swimming in flowers, Stanley's head thrown back, mouth idiot-open, bell clanging, turmoil of recess had already arrived; Yves Hermite calmly closes *Where The Red Fern Grows*. On the blacktop and now the sun has broken through clouds and for twenty desperate minutes, like twenty shafts shot into a pot of flesh, children screech from fence to fence entangled in a brutal social microcosm—birds in a tight and ugly cage swinging his fists bloodthirsty young eyes circle savagely around unmanageable limbs pants' seat dripping moist from black worm puddle cheeks salt-gouged eyes blood-darkened.

43.

The days of conjugal activity with his wife had ceased many years before, and the only activity that Harvey Shannon engaged in in bed, aside from sleeping, was reading slush manuscripts that had been sent into the Agency. Most of them, of course, were never read, but he was in the habit of grabbing a handful on his way out the door in the evening. It gave him a perverse satisfaction to see how inept writers were—to scan over those pages that were the hopes of the hopeless— energy put forward uselessly and postage wasted on pathetic dreams.

He found that, reading these, was one of the best cures for his insomnia, and also made him feel better about his own life, which was certainly no march of triumph.

The Shannon Agency, after all, was committed to books that mattered, books that engaged, enlightened, entertained. And, one thing was quite certain, the manuscript he had before him did none of those things. It was poorly written, and filled with juvenile filth.

His wife snored gently beside him, her body and head covered with blankets, only a few locks of her dyed-red hair visible.

He took a sip of water, placed the cup back on the nightstand, sighed, and then continued reading the repulsive pages before him:

"Unhand me!" I cried, turning to face my attackers.

I was not surprised in the least to find one of them being the henchman Mullo, who stood leering at me in the grossest possible manner. The other was the man whom I had seen the Duke conversing with when I first entered the dining room, a vagabond of small stature who glared at me with intelligent, evil eyes.

"When your master hears of this behavior, you won't get off with anything less than the gibbet," I exclaimed, trying to free myself from my bonds.

"Well, you'll have ample opportunity to complain to him," the smaller man said. "Step lively, for he is awaiting your presence."

Needless to say, I was startled by such uncongenial treatment, and at first assumed the cause to be my communing with the Duke's mother; the resultant bondage being the son's revenge. It soon became clear to me, however, that this was an altogether mistaken notion.

I was led down a lengthy series of steps and along a subterranean passageway decorated with ill-smelling mildews, a somewhat lower order of art than that which adorned the upper chambers. Small oaken doors, decayed with age, were placed somewhat randomly along the way. At the end of the passageway was a door, similar in appearance to the others, except that it was newer, larger and heavily girt with iron. On my approach, it was opened by an unseen hand and I was pushed through, the utmost force being applied to my backside.

I stood naked in a large, windowless chamber, ablaze with dancing orange torchlight. Skins of bears, leopards and other wild beast were laid en masse upon the floor, along with numerous rugs of exotic weave; the place was furnished in a grimly luxurious fashion; ghastly iron implements hung from the rough-hewn stone walls. The Duke sat before me, on an exquisitely carved chair upholstered with velvet, placed in the center of the room like a throne, his costume changed for a uniform of glossy black leather, well-studded with gems. The Countess was sprawled on a couch to my left, her white locks spilling over her breasts, which in that light had the hue of wounded flesh.

She smiled pertly when my pleading eyes met hers, which shone with Paphian vivacity.

The Duchess was seated to my right, on a low wooden stool, her gaze concentrated on the floor, apparently unwilling to rise to mine. Behind her, chained to the wall, their faces twisted with fear, were two men in sacerdotal garments. The midget, Rogero, frolicked around them and poked them with a silver-handled riding crop, probably belonging to his master.

I turned to the Duke.

"This is a rather singular interpretation of the rules of hospitality," I said, in as composed a manner as I could, nodding towards the two roughs behind me who had torn me from my bed.

"Oh, I am a true lover of the unique," the Duke lisped. "But, as I see it, you have little reason to complain. You were fatted on a fair supper, entertained with wine and music sweet, thrown into ecstasies I dare say you have never felt before by my very own mother, and now, all be it you have been handled by somewhat uncouth hands, the diversions will continue, in a grand style." He stood up and flourished his arm towards the two men, who hung by their chains, mouths agape in misery. "These priests, like yourself," he said, in a high tone. "These priests, like yourself, happened upon my castle—late in the afternoon of yesterday. They knocked at the door, begging funds in order to pay ransom for the release of Christians imprisoned by the Saracens. I promised them gold if they would but comply with a few simple requests. As ill luck would have it, they have taken my propositions to be not to their liking. I am thus impelled to use other measures to gain my will. Rogero, enough baiting!" he cried to the prancing manikin. "Mullo, Ludovico, the pilliwinks for the old one. His fingers appear to be itching the most."

The two roughs loosened the shackles of the older of the two priests, a somewhat plump man with cropped white hair, shaven atop, and a mouth possessed of the contours of a horse-shoe.

"This devil looks as if he has been using the funds he begs for purposes other than those he proposes," the Duke snickered. "Why, look at that belly! And in a time when famine is fast on the land! What a shame." And turning to me: "You should have seen him at the meal I provided. Such an immoderate wolf could hardly be fathomed. Leave it to the priesthood to breed those manners, to be sure."

The man stuttered out some inarticulate words of apology as Ludovico applied the pilliwinks to his fingers, which soon cut short his power of coherent speech altogether, turning the only sounds he could utter into cries of the most impassioned agony.

"Tighter," the Duke said.

The devices were tightened further. In the process, I distinctly heard the bones of his fingers crack. Groans of profound anguish filled the chamber. The poor fellow yelped like a dog, and then fell to the floor devoid of consciousness.

The Countess von Strobe tittered. The Duchess still sat, immobile as a statue, staring at her own feet.

The Duke turned to the other priest, who was younger and thinner. "So, my friend, do you wish to comply?"

"I . . . I cannot," the man stammered, his jaw quivering with fear. "It is forbidden."

"Summon Miss Vronsky with my little pet," the Duke told Ludovico. "Revive this old glutton," he commanded Mullo.

The entire scene disgusted me. Though honor bound me to help the poor men, I could do nothing in my condition as mutual prisoner. I begged the Duke to have pity, but he merely laughed, his gouged out cheeks supremely defined in the torchlight, and looked upon me with bright, mirthful eyes.

When Miss Vronsky walked in, she carried a cage in one hand and a large burlap sack in the other. A sour, wild-eyed cock strutted about the cage, its head moving in rapid, pendulous motions.

"Here you are, Duke," the woman said, setting down the goods and curtsying,—an absurd affectation under the circumstances.

The Baroness was visibly trembling. I thought I saw her hand move to her eyes and dash something away; a motion which prompted me to believe that she was not culpable concerning the circumstances, and sat thus against her will.

"Mullo, proceed!" the Duke commanded in a peevish, brutal tone.

The old priest lay upon the ground, his robes soaked through, an appalling, mystified expression highlighting the agony of his face. Mullo thrust him inside the sack and then, opening the cage, lured the tense cock in after, securing the opening with a length of cord. A scuffle ensued, led by a frantic rapacious crowing. Dreadful cries issued forth from the heart of the violently stirring bundle. The Duke, his nude mother, and the midget

Rogero, thoroughly relished the episode, each expressing their delight in a series of gleeful shouts and claps. The Countess von Strobe, the very woman I had lain with not an hour before, threw her head back and, opening her mouth of backward-drawn teeth, let out an uncontrolled laughter that would have been well suited had she been witnessing some absurd and comic farce.

After a time, the activity of the sack began to dwindle, and then it finally ceased. Mullo and Ludovico removed the load, and all that remained was a pasty black stain on the pelt where it had lain. The midget Rogero rolled on the floor, giggling madly and gnawing upon his riding crop.

The Duke smiled at the little beast.

"Miss Vronsky," he said. "Brandy for Mother and I—and our guest the Marquis as well."

"I cannot presume to drink, naked and roped like a criminal as I am," I cried, turning around.

"Sit beside me, my favorite," the Countess said, grabbing me and pulling me down beside her. "I will see that your lips stay moist."

She pressed her naked self against mine and, when the brandy was brought, gave me the first sip, before licking at the glass herself. The Duke found the scene to his taste and laughed much. The younger priest, who still remained chained in his most uncomfortable posture, wore a countenance of absolute dread. Undoubtedly, in his abstemious life, he had never witnessed such scenes of ruthless revel.

"So," said the Duke, turning to him, "are you willing to do as I request?"

"I will do what you wish," the priest said in a choked voice, apparently wishing not to synchronize his fate to that of his unfortunate companion.

"Unshackle him," the Duke commanded.

Mullo, who had just then returned with Ludovico, complied.

"Unrobe him," the Duke commanded.

Mullo tore the cassock from the man.

The priest stood, a pale, ill-kept thing, trembling though the room was tiresome hot, ablaze with torch fire.

"Wife of mine," said the Duke.

The Duchess rose and, with graceful movements, removed her rich garments, shedding them at her feet like the petals of a Dutch tulip. I drank in her body with my eyes. Though it was slim of design, it lacked not in the contours which fit a woman so well and are prone to set that which is in the breast of a man dancing. With a serious face, she approached the priest, touched, and began to stroke his body, which shook as if a hungry tiger were licking his skin. She set about trying to rouse the slack fellow, but whether through her own desire or her husband's sick fancies I know not.

"Oh, he is worthless," little Rogero sneered, skipping around the two. "How spry I would be if I were he!"

"He needs a woman with more crack to her whip to set him a bucking," the Countess von Strobe said, rising from the couch and strolling forth.

The Duchess withdrew to one side while the Countess proceeded to enwrap him in the rippling flesh of her full body, burying her tongue deep in his throat, and, with grip prehensile, doing complete violence to the root. At first the fellow cried out with undisguised agony, but, not the least to my surprise, he soon succumbed to the advances, sighing deeply and letting his hands wander, probably for the first time, where his mind had no doubt wandered a thousand times before.

The Duke, laughing lasciviously into his glass, signaled his wife to take the place of his mother, and I could not help but admire, to a certain degree, his perversion, which was nothing less than inspired.

The mild Duchess resumed her task, now made easier by the priest's open willingness to join in the sport. Indeed, his cooperation was unrestrained. Wearing a visage twisted with lust, like that of a Satyr, he toppled her to the floor. He proceeded with an exceptionally robust attitude, the vehemence of his actions showing clearly his design, which was to level the fortress, take no prisoners and leave the place sauced with the blood of his enemies. When his recklessness neared its height, the Countess, who stood nearby, snatched the riding crop from the hand of Rogero and began to flog the metamorphosed priest with singing strokes, the man crying out with undisguised joy at the snap of each violent contact. His body quaked with spasms. He screamed terribly and turned over, a naked slab of white, seemingly bloodless flesh extended on the floor. The Countess, who had apparently not derived ample satisfaction from being the mere instrument of his apex, threw aside the crop and flung herself upon him, as a bird of prey might a mouse, her full figure completely smothering his thin, insignificant frame.

44.

I fell out and onto the floor and moved across. I called and no one came, but I needed to get there. I needed to get there and started going, going across the floor smooth under me. "I'm Leaena," I thought. "I'm Leaena;" remembering *once I fell in water and another time fire.*

It was too far; it was too far and me needing to, because I don't fly like a bird. I'm Leaena; I don't fly like a bird. I crawled and stopped and pulled them off.

the sea filling up around me

It was whipping around and coming through the window. I could see blue on the floor and felt it coming in.

It came up and in; and I took it in.

She rolled me over and wiped and cleaned up. Then she was gone and it tickled me in there. I whispered and said what I felt. It got hot and I threw away the sheets, wondering *if my nose was cut off and burnt to ashes.*

Then there was light and I heard mumbling and then her on the stairs, going down from her room. I looked out the window. It was open and I looked out at the yard and the dried leaves. I remembered rolling in the dried leaves, how I used to like to roll in the dried leaves. There was the sound of her coming back upstairs.

I went. It was hot. There were the leaves outside and I watched the leaves.

I felt one in my nose. It moved out and hung in front of my lip. It dropped to the floor and the others started moving and coming out.

I heard it flush in the other room and then he came in. He was a white cheese. He did not have his shirt on and he was a white cheese.

45.

Rusty Maddox stood on the platform, absolutely exposed to the light of day, yet not the sun, which was low and concealed by a gray city sky.

The local came and he entered the last car. He saw and was seen. He could not sit and did not sit, but the initial leg of his commute was short. A bad odor lingered in the air, yet he was uncertain if it came from him or another. He had, earlier, showered and deodorized the pits of his arms, brushed his teeth, gargled mouthwash and shaved. He could do no more than this, or so he thought. With no place to sit, he stood, holding the vertical rail. A young woman also held the rail and her hand touched his. Instinctively, he moved his hand away and just as instinctively regretted it. He saw her shoes, which contained feet, and her dress, which hid her legs. The shoes, which were high-heeled, produced a complex phenomenon.

At 61 St. he crossed the platform and entered the express train, an express train, which pulled up more or less simultaneously with the local, which until he left was his. The express train was more crowded, by far.

The people were no longer human. Once again he held the rail. A man shorter than himself stood before him, very near, and his hair smelled like pistachio nuts.

It was times like these that Rusty felt that maybe he should have listened to his father, should have taken his advice.

The train was in the tunnel. The dirty walls were outside and the vibration from the tracks, steel rolling over steel, ascended into his bones.

At Grand Central Station he left the train. The Third Avenue exit was closed due to repairs, so the other exits were very crowded. A woman collapsed on the steps up, spraining her ankle, yet neither he nor any other person stopped, not to help her or to laugh in her face.

He took the Fifth Avenue exit and crossed the street in front of the United States Post Office. A long line of traffic receded into the distance in either direction and people of the city wove through and along the sidewalks. He walked over to Third Avenue and then into the building where he worked—where he had worked since graduating from university. The guard at the desk in the lobby said good morning to him.

"Good morning," Rusty replied, becoming once again an individual.

He took the elevator up to the eighth floor. Not directly, because others had piled into the elevator and disengaged at lower floors. A woman looked at him and compressed her lips in what was meant to be a smile. He bared his teeth and a sound came from his mouth.

"Good morning, Geri," Rusty said as he walked into the office.

Geri Robin, Junior Agent, was pouring herself a cup of coffee from the coffee pot. Growing up, she had had a love for stories, all sorts of stories, particularly those with international settings, unique subcultures, and multi-dimensional characters, and now, confronted with this situation, she repeated, almost word for word what Rusty had said. "Mr. Shannon wants to see you," she, Geri, added.

Rusty Maddox took off his coat, hung it up and put his messenger bag away. Turning on his computer, according to, amongst other things, habit, he was filled with a sense of comfort, yet also absolutely aware of impending catastrophe. He heard the sound of horns from the street, as well as a pigeon cooing on the windowsill.

"Life in the city," he thought.

He then went to the office of the Founder and President of the Agency, Mr. Shannon. As he entered the door the taste of dog food filled his mouth, from the back forward. He had never eaten dog food, but canned corned beef, which, he imagined, was probably very similar in taste.

"You wanted to see me?" he asked.

Harvey Shannon explained that there had been a comingling of manuscripts on his desk which had been causing him no little confusion.

"Foreign rights . . . film and television," Mr. Shannon said, "I can't tell which is which."

Rusty noted that Mr. Shannon's upper lip was glistening with a thin film of sweat. He, Rusty Maddox, ran his tongue over his own upper lip and was disappointed that there was no salty taste. He felt the texture of his shaved whiskers, but this was without pleasure. He would have liked to have scratched himself, but did not.

He went to the men's restroom to urinate but no urine projected from him. All the same he washed his hands, drying them with a leaf of brown paper torn from the receptacle. "What a shock," he thought, without being fully convinced, or directly connecting the sequence of events that led up to that moment.

"I need a vacation," he thought. "Badly."

Later, that is to say shortly after 5 p.m., he put on his coat, took up his messenger bag and left the office. Outside, he stood on the curb and watched the traffic pass. The light turned green and he crossed Third Avenue. At Grand Central Station he boarded the 7 train. It was empty, not totally empty, but there were very few people. Then he did not think but saw without clarity. That a man with no arms, a can hanging from around his neck, walked in front of him made no difference. He, without arms, was a beggar of money, one, thankfully, apart from him, and even in that moment, Rusty Maddox knew nothing of him, but wondered if that man were to touch him, would his own arms fall off?

"I should write a poem about this," he thought. "Why am I so frightened?"

Getting off the train he walked down steps, off the raised platform. At home he made himself a salami sandwich and ate it while sitting on the couch. As he ate the sandwich he noticed that his feet tapped in rhythm with his chewing. He then rose from his seat and went to the dresser. From beneath a stack of white, or very nearly white men's underwear he took out a packet of a mysterious substance.

He picked one of his nostrils, an absent-minded expression on his face.

The words seemed to sit in space for a moment before they were gone.

This time, in the privacy and comfort of his own bathroom, the urine projected freely. Afterwards, he shook his penis and re-inserted it into the flap of his underwear. The mirror showed him a young man with lusty, intelligent eyes, and twisted lips.

46.

Jae-yong drove fast and his car hugged the bends and gravel shot out from beneath his tires. It was a beautiful late fall day and the sky was a pure blue. The layered hills were dotted with yellow flowers. Hawkbeard and cholla cactus clung near the road, mostly of a rich forest green, some bunches or arms dried to skeleton, a dull gray. High up on one hill a cross was laid out in white stones and to his left, on the verge of a precipice, a wooden crucifix was planted with fresh flowers set before it.

He found where Amy lived; an old mud building of three rooms surrounded by wattle fencing; laundry hanging in the yard three-days dry, now dusty and dirty. A creek ran off to one side of the house, forming a fissure of green that wound into the distance. Behind the place rose the open, high desert country; strokes of dark blue mountains could be made out in the distance.

Azra answered the door saying, "Amy's not here."

They went inside and both sat down at the kitchen table.

He was closer and kissed her.

"You're rubbing up against me," she said.

What had been stirred moved faster and spread out and it was like a hurricane of gelatin.

He looked over and saw her face. When he had dressed and gone into the kitchen she was there making a pot of coffee. They sat and drank coffee and smoked cigarettes and when Amy came through the back door neither of them spoke but each looked cold and unemotional.

"I didn't figure seeing you around here so soon," Amy said. "What have you got? I've been having the fever. You don't know how bad I've been having it. I keep telling myself if I just knew a good chemist everything would be okay."

She was dressed in army fatigues, and her hair tied back in a ponytail, thin and ratlike. There was that vague and merciless look in her eyes that mirrored something dark in his own soul and produced an aura of general unease.

Jae-yong took a Ziploc bag of white powder out of his pocket and handed it to her.

"This is what I've been looking for," Amy said, dipping a moistened pinkie inside the bag and tasting it.

Amy emptied a small pile onto an old newspaper and went in the back room.

"She's all worked up over that powder," he said.

"You brought it to her."

Jae-yong looked into Amy's eyes. They were rolled back in her head and only the whites, which were not white but a dull yellow, showed. Amy did not look alive. Her skin was gray and her breathing was hard to perceive. She lay sprawled in a chair, the works—a Becton-Dixon syringe and a blackened spoon—sat on a nearby coffee table along with other paraphernalia. Her thin body was taut and motionless, the ponytail, like that of a rat, curled out from behind her head onto one shoulder.

"I must have used too much pool cleaner," Jae-yong thought.

"Should we bury her?" asked Azra.

"She isn't dead."

"There's a creek," Azra said. "If we put her in the creek she might wake up."

They dragged Amy down to the creek and sat her in the water. It was very clear and shallow and watercress and moss grew up to and along the bank and they laid her head against the bank. Cottonwoods grew and formed shade and, without speaking, they listened to the water as it rippled over Amy.

47.

Bearded women, dripping orange vomit. Sucking on his mother's nipple. The other children fill their sunken cheeks with what lies before them, shouting, masticating in a feeble frenzy.

Stanley's skin, blanched by bedroom darkness, melts beneath bright sun and ruptures in contact with twigs, blacktop and nature's abrasive arsenal. Balls crashing against skulls, bludgeoned by fists, a frantic wave of insects. Stanley lunges ineffectually, trips, gravitates toward suffering and shame, humiliation of years, not mere moments, he is a crown of thorns. Razors etching gore on his delicate pelt. Scratching seconds are needles pinning children like beetles, minutes red-hot pokers piercing body end to end. Pray to be an hour older, pray for relenting blue shelter, the freedom of streets, the melting of the social cage misery mutates to pathetic joy, shouts, red, yellow, hurdling sound. Stanley is jacketed and making his way toward the exit, the colorful door, yet he hears his name called out, huskily, repeated, Yves Hermite calling it out; now empty of all true sound and Yves Hermite tells Stanley that he

has something that he has been wanting to talk to him
discuss never mind that Yves Hermite is drawing curtains camouflage weighing out some ground squirrel or
a roasted armadillo
so love the worms
and red fungus;
and then confirm
you are shameless
roll in the mud
and eat the hay,
don't be timid
at this buffet.

48.

Geometric aesthetics. The Pantheon of: M-AGRIPPA-
L-F-COS-TER-TIVM-FECIT   PANTHEVM
VETVSTATIE CORRVPTVM RESTITVERTVNT
Sphinx of the Campus Martius, with its simple structure, its perfect, airy cupola, was a masterpiece of classical art. There were the works of Giovanni Bernini,
Baroque   the illusion: false perspective   trompe-
l'oeil   those great architects of long ago: Iktinos,
Rabrius, Pytheos, Hermogenes, Vitruvius, Apollodo-
rus, Severus, Celar   Yoshimitsu (his timber-framed
Golden Pavilion) & Fujiwara Yorimichi & Sinan, the
greatest of Ottoman designers; his search for a homog-
enous interior   Sangallo, Bramante   Villard de Hon-
necourt   Isidoros, the Hagia Sophia, that perfection
of the Byzantine; complicated, bold

a place where gods could be worshipped, emperors
dwell and multitudes endure initiation   a cella[r]
where some cult statue might belong; Phidias' great
Zeus, chryselephantine Athena

the eyes, accusatory, and shot with desperate light, stared up at him and the lips quivered

crocodile-headed Sobek

the eyes did not move. A thin strand of saliva threaded out of the mouth and broke away onto the floor. There was dullness once more and the apparent recognition an illusion; the woman remained almost allegorical in her representation of greed, hate, pain and abused lust

sinkholes. water draining into limestone cavities joined to continuous underground river. stirring sideways between layers of rock seeping liquid dissolve and enlarge drop. drain   entering rooms and passages deposit calcium carbonate dripstone features   what took nature millions to do; for nothing could match the supreme and random exactness of water.

Sequences of arches (ultra-archaic Doric stalactites, sub-geometric Ionic stalagmites, dripping Aeolic capitals), vaulted chambers jointly following all the true rules of both Mnesicles and Taoism, making use of the naked body of nature, her caressing uneven curves, easy, gradual buttressing and grand vaulting

he walked through the dark room, out the back door and into the light. The slope was under his feet and he stepped from foothold to foothold, avoiding the patches of cholla cactus and the other small cactus that sat sunk in the dry earth. The view rolled out on all sides, bubbles of reddish earth dotted with sparse growth, in the middle-distance certain hills rising like young and erect breasts behind which loomed the blue block of mountains to one side and, to the other, the atmosphere, veiled saw blade of peaks.

The earth was uneven and full of gulches where the water flowed when the rain came and made the rock smooth. Aside from cactus, there was much yucca and the dried pods stuck out from the nests of sharp leaves

those Graeco-Roman-Oriental elements he shattered and reconstituted according to the natural laws of geology.

his hands were in the dirt and his chest was very cold and heavy

he could feel the wet and the cold inside him and remembered all the times. There were people out in the world who moved and talked and lived and the rocks and the sand were real

I was on my hands and crawled across the grass, the switch ringing against my back and a whimpering coming from my mouth. I could feel my eyes wet and burning. He loomed there, lashing, against my cheeks and forehead and everywhere. I screamed out for help, but no one heard me or cared. Everything was still flying in my head. Jae-yong stepped on the butt of his cigarette.

My feet kept moving and moving. My heart bumped and bumped in my chest.

"Jae-yong, please, leave me alone."

He told me that he didn't want to leave me alone and started to move towards me.

49.

Mother, do not think that I cannot remember, when you were young and a handsome woman. How you pampered me, and showed me the tools to live by.

Your little boy was not always befriended by his classmates; but by you, I was always adored. Those memories will be cherished, wherever the wind takes me, blows me—be it Asia, or the deserts of Arabia—in all places I will live by your teachings, and let the wind's pressure recall a mother's caress.

You have treated me too well; but I will not blame you—for everything I have become. Yes, tinker or tailor, we all must bear the burdens—and oh, how I know you have yours—and desires.

For the old oak is still verdant. And there are some small birds who find comfort on its branches, and squirrels that store nuts in its boughs.

Forgive me if, when the winter comes, I gather up the dead wood of neighboring trees for my fuel—I know very well that you would never let your son grow cold or hungry—and know, that you are my only shade.

50.

Yves Hermite was a man with candid blue eyes and an invisible past. He had fallen in with Aunt Min-jung while she was traveling in Mexico. Prowling the same beach at Puerto Escondido, the tide frothing beside them, they met. He was staying on one end of the playa, in a grass bungalow, sleeping in a hammock; she at the other, in a four-star hotel with security at the gate. They were thrown together; the man apparently fascinated her. Aunt Min-jung was very generous to those few she formed an affection for. She had feelings for Yves Hermite and made him her parasite. It was impossible to say whether her feelings for him were platonic, or more. But she did choose to adopt him; she did not marry him.

When she passed away in mystery while voyaging through Calabria with her "son," Jae-yong did not know quite what to say. It seemed too absurd that the rogue would murder her. A private investigator was hired, but no solid case formulated. There was no evidence to go by. She had fallen into a ravine while hiking around Aspromonte. Hermite claimed that he had tried to save her, but failed. Many accidents happened in that area, so it was fully possible that his story was true. Many murders happened in that area, so it was fully possible that his story was false.

Aunt Min-jung left her affairs in disorder. There was a will in which her house and the bulk of her estate were bequeathed to Jae-yong, and a second, written up by her lawyer not long before her demise, which left the property evenly divided between himself and Hermite. The Yeon family rebelled at the idea of Yves Hermite coming into possession of anything. He was obviously an adventurer!

51.

amnesia granules
a third mesh
searching the ground
I swallow my water
I wait
blades tickling
this is not all my imagination
the next looking at each one closely and with serious
consideration he noticed the curvatures of her as they
faced his eyes with their glistening bidding him come
fling on the floor forcing her open bloody feathers, red
and swollen urges continually corrupted he only knew
that being alone with one made him long to hear lusty
agony

52.

EXTERIOR. DAY.

The camera lens clears to the sidewalk of a crowded street in San Francisco. It focuses in low, so that we can only see the feet of the passersby. To the screen's right we can see the bottom half of a popsicle vendor's cart. Music plays on the soundtrack—a toccata by Conrad Friedrich Hurlebusch. We see Jae-yong's feet approach the popsicle stand. The camera pans up. We see Jae-yong buying a popsicle. He walks down the street eating the popsicle, amidst the crowd. He looks in shop windows, at shoes, teapots, purses, fishing rods, etc. He finishes the popsicle and tosses the stick in the gutter. He crosses the street. A man with only one arm is walking towards him. Jae-yong walks exaggeratedly out of the man's way, a nervous tick on his face. He turns down a street and walks. He stops in front of a large residential building. It is Mrs. Cheng's. He walks up the steps which are lined with coffee cans filled with cigarette butts. The porch has old chairs and a couch on it. Sitting on the couch is a man with a beard and thick glasses. He has a small radio in one hand that emits extremely staticky country music. The man looks at Jae-yong, blinking. Jae-

yong nods at the man and knocks on the door. The man doesn't respond, only blinks. Mrs. Cheng opens the door, smiling affectedly. She is a woman in her late sixties.

MRS. CHENG: How are you doing, Mr. Yeon? I'm glad to see you back so soon.

JAE-YONG: It's nice to see you too. I just came to see Stanley.

MRS. CHENG: Yes, yes, he is in his room. If you look in his room I believe you will be very happy.

JAE-YONG [*smiling weakly*]: Thanks.

[JAE-YONG *walks towards the stairs.*]

HIGH-SHOT OF JAE-YONG WALKING UP THE STAIRS.
He goes down a dark hallway lined with doors. We can hear the sounds of drills and thrusting movements as well as dull laughter. A number of photos of wild animals flash before us: rhinoceros, apes, tigers, etc. Arriving at Stanley's door he taps gently.

STANLEY [*from within*]: Come in.

STANLEY'S ROOM.
We see Stanley from Jae-yong's POV. He is lying on his bed, arms behind head. The walls of the room are covered with paintings, modern and very good, though put up

with little care. Close-ups of sections of the paintings flash
soundlessly over the screen. Phallic. Vulvic.

JAE-YONG: Stanley?

STANLEY: Jae-yong.

JAE-YONG: Are they treating you okay here, Stanley?
The women aren't giving you too many problems?

STANLEY [*sitting up on his bed*]: No, I'm doing fine,
Yeon Jae-yong. If there are any women, they leave
me alone, but I wish someone would touch me.

[*Stanley grins. Jae-yong casually walks over to one of the
many small paintings on the wall.*]

CLOSE-SHOT OF PAINTING.

53.

The large gold fountain pen sped across the page:

> *. . . it was hardly that I was in love with her, but simply because I was so damnably broke. When we met I was literally starving. There I was, in Puerto Escondido, poorer than any of the Mexicans. It was rather ridiculous. Certainly there were many delicious boys, but I did not have the funds to procure them. I needed a patron badly, and there she was, such an obvious old maid, an apple just waiting for a worm like me. Of course she did not have the foggiest idea——*

Yves Hermite's door was open. He heard the distant sound of several voices, footsteps on the parquet floor downstairs. He set down the fountain pen and stood up.

"This lack of privacy is disgusting," he murmured. He quickly tossed a sheet of blank paper over his letter, left the room and trod downstairs, where he could see Jae-yong and Samir at the entrance taking off their jackets and handing them to Giancarlo.

"Oh, nice to see you back!" Yves Hermite cried, waving his hand.

Jae-yong looked up in surprise. "Are you still here?" he said.

"Come now, there is no reason why we both can't live——"

"To hell with you."

Yves Hermite smiled.

"I just want to share," he said. "We can both live here, can't we? I don't think I am being so difficult. If you knew how long it has been since I have had a home of my own."

Yves Hermite winked.

Samir nodded his head.

Jae-yong walked out the front door without bothering about his jacket. He walked into the sunlight, a curious figure, with close-fitting black trousers, a white linen shirt and a lime green tie. Samir jogged after him. The two men strolled across the impeccable lawn; the weather humid; the sky white. Jae-yong took a pair of sunglasses from his pocket and put them on.

"Shall we get a drink?" Samir asked.

"Yes. But not here."

"Clearly."

They were soon driving towards Great Neck in Samir's car.

"Here?" he asked.

"It looks like a dive."

"All the better."

Inside they ordered whisky sours and sat at a table near a curtained window. It was still only mid-afternoon, and the place was nearly empty. A few old men were perched on stools at the counter and two young women sat at the opposite end of the room, near the jukebox, laughing and talking in loud, uncultured voices.

"How is your drink?"

"Disgusting. Yours?"

"Repulsive."

"These are the kind of experiences that give me neuralgia."

"Well, we don't have to stay too long."

Jae-yong noticed that one of the young women was grimacing in his direction. It was the curse of his good looks, of taste in dress and manner. Inevitably it attracted many, and vulgarians were often enough stimulated by his charms. He lit a cigarette and passed his cigarette case to Samir. The grimacing girl rose from her seat and walked towards them, and presently troubled them for a light.

"Thanks. Don't I know you?"—to Jae-yong—"You look familiar."

"Turkey?"

"I've never been there."

"Laos?"

"Phou Khoun?"

"The Sala Guest House . . . three years ago. You were wearing high-waisted pink trousers and an elaborate textile shawl."

"But not for long."

"Leyli?"

"That's right. Looking for ongoing respectful fun. Kind-hearted, artistic, and affectionate. . . . And here comes my friend."

The other woman, who was quite small, had come limping up. She squinted at Jae-yong and smiled.

"Delphilia?"

CUT TO: INTERIOR. THE WATERFALL ROOM AT THE EDGEWOOD MOTEL. NIGHT.

The room is ill-lit, and the little light there is glints off the mirrored ceiling. Bodies are sprawled out on the bed in their underwear or naked. A giant air-brushed painting of a leopard decorates the wall. In one corner a waterfall is gurgling mysteriously. The camera pans in on Delphilia's face, which is poetic and expressive.

DELPHILIA: Pleasure is so ephemeral. Will anyone want me when I am but a salad of bones, when the sun has grown cold and the moon has fallen from the sky?

SPIRIT OF AN ANCIENT SAGE: Things appear and recede moment by moment, so how can one expect to find longevity in the delights of the flesh?

DELPHILIA: I long to find someone to care for me, but every day I'm abandoned anew. What will happen when I no longer want to give these pieces?

SPIRIT OF ALICE PAUL: Depend on yourself. Have no faith in the sex that is opposed to your own.

DELPHILIA: Looking at pig faces fill me with such disgust. Looking over at my lover I feel as if I am truly the luckiest girl in the world. He is like a fine stallion; the more he is adored, the more he prances and neighs.

JAE-YONG: Shall we kiss again?

DELPHILIA: Kiss?

JAE-YONG: Kiss . . . and . . .

DELPHILIA: Lips . . .

LEYLI [*in a very loud, theatrical voice*]: And afterwards we can virginally smoke cigarettes and stare at each other, stricken with deep loneliness. Our eyes are the main culprits; but Delphilia's hands are small and soft, closely resembling those of van Scorel's *Maria Magdalena* which express an ideal of femininity, and her lips are like a burst pomegranate and her nose alone is enough to make any man's heart flutter, with its slightly upturned elegance and straight, narrow deportment. One generally only finds such noses on the great women of history, such as Cleopatra, whose nose it's told could easily conquer a nation on its own!

DELPHILIA: And my squint?

JAE-YONG: Very erotic!

CUT TO: INTERIOR. THE ROOM NEXT-DOOR.
There are no lights on, so the room is almost completely black, aside from the little light that is let in through the curtained window.

ALEX: Maurice?

MAURICE: Yes, Alex.

ALEX: I thought this was supposed to be a vacation.

MAURICE: It was supposed to be, Alex. It really was.

CUT TO: MOUNT KEMUKUS. JAVA. EXTERIOR.
We see strangers meeting and then wandering off under trees to perform sex. Some mount atop each other like dogs, others twist their bodies in complex, ritualistic postures. The sound of their grunting is veiled by the rich song of exotic birds which are perched in the trees.

54.

I tripped downstairs with a light step, and, after wandering through some unpeopled halls and chambers, at last found the dining room, sparkling with the scintillas of dozens of candles, an inviting, linen-covered table ranged in the center.

The Duke was stationed off to one side, giving instructions to a servant. When he saw me, he approached with brisk steps, followed by his wife and mother, who were just then entering. He was tall and remarkably thin, with gouged out cheeks and a head of thick, black, overly pomaded hair. His dress was immaculate, being made up of a violet waist-coat of the latest cut, ochre pantaloons that stretched dapperly over his firm legs, and a good deal of costly lace tastefully adorning his collar and cuffs. We shook hands and exchanged the formalities of introduction.

"You have already met my lovely wife," he said, in a cultivated voice. "This other beautiful woman is my mother, the Countess von Strobe."

The Countess bowed slightly, but did not offer her hand. She was of the most rigid Germanic type, but was none the less remarkably attractive for her years, which could not have been less than fifty.

"But let us not keep our guest waiting any longer," the Duchess said, smiling faintly. "He must be famished after his journey."

The meal was served by the same Russian woman who had shown me to my room. I was surprised that the Duke, a man of obvious wealth, did not have an especial set of servants for the purpose; even more surprised was I when I witnessed the alacrity with which the woman performed her various tasks, seeming to be in all places at once, now filling a glass with wine on one side of the table, now serving up a dish on the next, all the while maintaining the same stone-like composure which I had first noted in her.

"I hope you like venison," the Countess remarked, showing a set of even, inward-curving teeth that would have done credit to any member of the English peerage.

"Indeed I do," I replied in my most affable manner, setting knife and fork to work.

Her cold blue eyes pierced me for a moment before she in turn proceeded to partake of the chop before her, cutting off bits and inserting them in her mouth with precision. I felt my foot toyed with beneath the table. The Countess was across from me and I smiled affably.

We supped richly and drank of good wine. The Duke's conversation was refined and intelligent; he expressed his views with graceful diction and I, in turn, gave proof that I was no stranger to the art of sleek banter. The Countess was severe and, though not especially talkative, in no way relaxed her foot play. The Duchess was dainty and silent as a nun.

"Do you enjoy music?" asked the Duke when the meal had reached its end. "I am so used to being the only male at table, that I have grown into the habit of forsaking custom and retiring to the drawing-room with the women, rather than lingering over my wine alone."

"I personally much prefer mixed company to that of only men," said I as we rose and moved in a body towards the drawing-room. "Which of the ladies will honor us with a recital this evening?"

The Duke guffawed. "My dear fellow," he said, "I hardly consider the mincing of a grown woman at a piano to be entertainment. I cannot tolerate amateurs."

Needless to say, this rather arrogant boast peaked my curiosity. I wondered what sort of musician the Duke had in his service; whether it were some magnificent artist he had imported from Thuringia, or one of the great masters of my own land of Italia, lured into these cold regions with promise of gold.

We walked into a drawing-room decorated entirely in red damask the designs of which, on close inspection, revealed themselves to be of a rather naughty variety. But, as these images only presented themselves when light hit them at the proper angle, they came and went as puerile, somewhat liquorish phantasms, without staying long enough for the mind to penetrate their significance.

We seated ourselves upon the roseate, ornately-carved furniture, the Duke and I each with a glass of fine brandy in one hand and a cigarillo in the next, the ladies poised in prim expectation.

"Rogero!" the Duke called, ringing a bell.

The door opened and a midget walked in, decked

from head to foot in an outlandishly ruffed costume of the boldest plum blossom hue, a guitar of proportion equal to his height (which could not have been above three foot), lingering in his hands. He bowed.

"A song for our guest, Rogero," the Duke commanded, with a broad, luscious smile, his lips wet with liquor.

Rogero bowed again. He strummed his guitar and sang:

> Bloody games he loves;
> His spirit's decayed;
> It's filled with hot
> And rotting lust
>
> He'll make you his steed,
> He'll make you bleed,
> On his vile sauce
> He'll make you feed
>
> Crazy gentleman,
> He's tall and thin;
> That master of vice,
> At intercourse he's wise
>
> Such a savage beast,
> Yes, you he'll tease;
> Crazy gentleman,
> The mad lord of sin

His voice was indeed that co-mingling of the sweet and the firm which brings pleasure to the ear, but I could not much abide by the lyrics, which were little more than the churlishness of a common guttersnipe.

He persisted:

> Crazy gentleman,
> How he loves to sin;
> In cold castle walls,
> That lord of love
>
> Your white flesh he wants,
> Yes, you he taunts,
> As he licks the sap
> From your wounds
>
> You he pierces with
> His hungry eyes;
> Yes, when you awake
> You'll get a ghastly surprise

"Bravo!" shouted the Duke, rising from his seat and giving approbation with a clapping of his hands. The ladies did likewise, though in a somewhat more restrained manner and, so as not to appear rude, I followed suit, setting down my glass, rising to my feet and giving a weak, "Fine, fine," whilst I set the skins of my palms gently against each other.

This unqualified encouragement had the immediate result of adding to the manikin's vigor. He smiled, showing a set of horse-like, dun-colored teeth, and, with a sudden gust of energy, began to dance around the room, a second song, thrice as rich as the first, ripe upon his lips.

184

55.

"You understand, Mrs. Yeon," said Mr. Taffe, "that, if you go ahead with this, Mr. Hermite will become a principal heir. . . . In other words, he will get half of your entire estate . . . your nephew the rest."

"I understand perfectly," replied Min-jung. "Yves has made me so happy. It's only right that he should get . . . something. . . . That boy loves me very much you see."

Mr. Taffe raised his eyebrows, saying, "I am only your lawyer ma'am. I can only advise you on legal transactions. . . . So I must say that, if I were in your position I would think more on the matter before making a final decision."

"No," she said, "I have thought it over enough. Draw up the papers and bring them to me tomorrow. I'll sign them and we'll be done with it. Yves will be grateful to me when I'm gone."

Taffe was about to comment on this statement when Mr. Hermite entered the room.

"Did I hear my name?" Hermite said. "I hope nobody was saying anything bad about me." He laughed. "I'm sensitive you know."

The expression on Taffe's face immediately betrayed his dislike for the man.

"What's up with you, Taffe?" said Yves Hermite, throwing himself down on the couch. "I didn't expect to see you here today. What's it all about, Min-jung dear? Nothing important is it?"

"Nothing you need to worry yourself about," she replied with a smile. And then turning towards Taffe: "So I will just need to sign the papers?"

"Yes," he replied rising from his seat, "I'll bring them by tomorrow."

"Going already?" said Yves. "Won't you stay for a drink?"

"No," replied Taffe, taking his leave, "I don't drink this early in the day. . . . I have to work you know."

When Min-jung and Yves were alone, Yves got up from his seat and, going over to the older woman, kissed her romantically on the lips.

That evening, after dining together, the "mother" and "son" sat in the living room drinking wine.

"I do love you so, Yves," said Min-jung, laying her gray head on the younger man's shoulder.

"Yes," he replied. "I love you madly."

"I'm not too old for you?"

"Too old? . . . No, not in the least. You're a mature, handsome woman."

"Handsome?"

"You're lovely," he said, smiling gently.

"Oh, Yves . . ."

"Min-jung . . ."

"Yes?"

"We should travel more."

"Didn't we just get back from Vancouver?"

"I would like to show you the world."

"Would you . . . darling? . . . It's very large."

". . . Italy . . ."

56.

FUCKING POMEGRANATES GROWING SHAD-
OWS AND SHADOWY FEELING THE SORCERY
OF THE BOTTOMLESS PIT SO I WILL STICK
MY TONGUE IN YOUR MAGNOLIAS EVEN
WITH THE BLOSSOMS DRY YOUR REPUL-
SION TOWARD THE MATING PROCESS
BUT YOU CAN FEEL MY MAMMAL SMALL
AMOUNTS OF ELECTRICAL INTERVENTION
MY JUPITERIAN THRUSTS TO SPIT PLASTIC
LOGS ILLUMINED BY A LIGHTBULB IN THIS
HUMAN SOUND MUSEUM GIVING A DEM-
ONSTRATION OF PRIMAL FEAR GUTTERAL
NASALS AND SUB-PALATAL RETROBELCHES
OF RAW FLESHED CUM EATEN BY MISTRESS-
ES AS THEY DEFECATED IN THE DIRT CHEW-
ING THE TOUGH MEAT UNTIL THE GRISLY
BONE SHOWED.

57.

Jae-yong is in his study. Several empty bottles, of both whisky and wine, are on his desk. A half-smoked joint sits in the ashtray and a stick of Mandala incense is burning in front of a small brass deity of mystical appearance. He is reading a book, the title of which is evident in coquelicot lettering: The Secret Manual of the Jade House.

JOE THE SKY: Jae-yong, quit indulging this way. There are many good books to read. You might find the *Ksānabhangasiddhi* quite entertaining.

YVES HERMITE: Don't listen to Joe. As Mother has always said, it is hard to trust a man with long hair.

JOE THE SKY: Spirit . . .

JAE-YONG: And what spirit would that be?

YVES HERMITE: God does not exist. The most beautiful things in this world are the exposed sexual organs of mammals.

JOE THE SKY: Jae-yong, eventually we will find happiness.

[*Alex enters whistling merrily. His hair is freshly curled and glistens with pomade. He has a large spaniel by his side and an unopened bottle of Champagne in his hand.*]

ALEX: Heel, boy! I believe this to be the spot where my rendezvous with Maurice is set for.

YVES HERMITE: [*aside*] True?

ALEX: I'll just rest myself under the shade of this fair desk until the lad cometh.

CUT TO: EXTERIOR. ENGLAND. DAY.
Several people, both men and women, stand completely naked in a green field bordered by lush woods. They hold bows and arrows and shoot the arrows at targets which are set up on one side of the field. The camera zooms in on mouths and eyes which show clear signs of arousal as the arrows hit their targets. Nipples. Throats. Hairy chest.

58.

there were the lilac bushes and he was behind them stomach like a whirlpool and arms drawn inside his shirt crossed hands feeling soft alcohol loose pectoral muscles he looked out through the foliage at the pure even morning light and did not think did not want to or dare to his eyes tired lower lip tucked beneath his moustache which thus almost ran down onto his neck without chin or lip to offset it from the rest of his body

yet not altogether displeasing to unfamiliar taste Leaena resolved herself would have a different practically every night schmucks drunken loafers seduced by slattern charm so why should he complain Anthony Quinn that Irish-Mexican actor the only man in theatre to have ever been able to realistically play an Italian a Greek and a Frenchman he saw those old Athenian contests for the drama prize the brute Ajax as he should be Rachel Félix and Louis Delaunay come down to us the former said to be the great woman who revived public appreciation of tragedy a strange man who continued playing seventeen-year-old lovers until he was past sixty

predominate sense of failure swirled around inside of him and he rose and batted dirt, dried leaves and twigs off the seat of his pants and came out onto the empty lot. There were beer cans scattered through the weeds and high green grass and pigweed. The trail led out to a dirt lot where cars were parked and then there was the paved road and people driving along it like the world was an absolutely safe and insoluble place, their faces absorbed in an apparent mirage of satisfaction far separate from the silent and ever-present turmoil that ran through it all.

He was unscrewing the fifth, but before the top even came off he was over in the weeds, everything coming out. Afterwards he took a drink of the fifth and then emptied half the cup of coffee onto the dirt and filled it the rest of the way from the fifth. He walked and drank the lukewarm liquor mixture and felt much better and opened the little pack of oatmeal cookies and dunked them in the mixture and ate them.

His thumb was out and his mind far away when the pick-up truck pulled alongside and the driver flicked his head back toward the bed of the truck. Samir climbed in and called out thanks and his destination, and then they were moving, him hunched up against the cab, the wind blowing through his hair and whistling in his ears. They turned and drove past the penitentiary, but he did not look over, just knew it was there like he always knew. It was something he dreamed of at night and remembered during the day and did not fear any more than a man fears death but did himself equate with death and all finality. Its towers stuck up from amidst the foreground of sagebrush, not ominously, just plainly and without mystery.

The road stretched out, winding through the low hills of cracked rock and dry dirt, cactus and cedar, and Samir could hear the sound of his feet as they ground the sand that lay between them and the blacktop. He looked ahead at the silent stripe of yellow that receded over the next dip in the road and reappeared much smaller further on as it wrapped itself around a bend of red-rock. From a distance behind him came the purr of tires and he slowly turned his body around, walked backward.

The passenger door swung open.

"Get in," Jae-yong said.

Jae-yong drove with his left hand on the wheel, his right laying limp on his lap.

"You too?"

"Yes."

He could feel a kind of whinnying pain as he said it and could hear the crunching in his neck as he turned his head away.

Jae-yong drove along the back roads, one hand on the steering wheel, eyes squinting from the smoke that curled before them.

Azra sat on the chopping block in front of the trailer. She smoked a hand-rolled cigarette and sat there while the dogs barked. By the way she started moving around on the chopping block he could tell that she was look-ing at him, and as Samir got out of the car he handed him six cigarettes and told him to give them to Azra.

59.

. . . *there she was in that bed, he kissed her cold unresponsive lips—those pained eyes telling him that she was already halfway in the other world.*

She went to the blood bank and donated plasma; to a strip joint to apply for work entered the darksmoke room, men brooding over bottles, made her leave without opening her mouth.

He made a little money selling methamphetamine. Leaena snorted the stuff. . . . He became disgusted with the way she ate, sat and toyed with her earlobe.

They found a few grams of methamphetamine on him, he bit an officer of the law, was tied to a stretcher, taken away writhing and screaming. They had to gag him. They had captured an animal, a dangerous hybrid that had best be kept under observation.

60.

THE BATHROOM OF A BAR. HIGH-SHOT OF
SAMIR IN A TOILET STALL. NIGHT.
*We hear loud music in the background. Samir shoots up
diamorphine. He leaves the toilet stall dragging his feet.*

BAR. FULL SHOT OF BAR FROM SAMIR'S POV.
*The camera is out of focus, weaving unevenly, giving us
the perspective of someone high on heroin. We see people
drinking and grinning. Painted mouths. Suggestive moustaches. A band is playing. They wear T-shirts and jeans
and all have long hair. As the camera moves through the
bar, heads turn in its direction.*

BAR. MEDIUM SHOT OF SAMIR.
*Samir moves through the bar. He can hardly walk; he stag-
gers, dragging his feet. People begin to stare. He approaches
a woman with a drink. He reaches out his hand as if to
take the drink from her and collapses on her. The woman
lets out a little shriek and pushes him away. He collapses
on the floor. A male voice shouts something incoherent.*

The band abruptly stops playing. People start talking (ad-lib), saying that Samir looks high, should they call an ambulance, etc. The camera close-ups on Samir's face and it's evident that he's dangerously high.

61.

When the plates broke, more than just a period of her life fell to pieces. Those lines that divided, demarked her as woman, citizen, and even human, were erased, leaving the one embodied being, sentient and hardly different from the jellyfish or other deep water, soft and flexible creature. It was no longer a matter of how many walls or how many rooms, about a door opening or a tear shedding. She remembered crossing the bridge and the wild ducks that flew out of the weeds.

"Where are they going?" she had asked herself.

Her initial attraction was unsupervised by experience—experience of his type; executorial, vain, selfish—a fair representation of his sex conjoined with his class—molded from the latter days of civilization; the merchant usurping the respect once gleaned by royalty; the odor of a somewhat decadent, but unnamable perfume.

"Use your head," he would tell her, as she used her body
forgetting
there were not two

dividing her, bubbles clinging to her skin. The water lapped against the edge of the tub. There was the periodic gurgle of the secondary drain, and, when her ears were below the surface, this resounded with remarkable depth, as if she were at the bottom of the ocean.

She opened her eyes and looked down at the elongation of her body. She found nothing wrong with it; her oldest friend

sound joined with

a rush of cold air

and countenance dull, insolent.

"Excuse me," Stanley said. "I need to use the bathroom."

Her legs were clasped tightly together and arms sheltered her chest.

His eyes looked on, with a kind of sluggish degeneracy.

"I'm going to use the restroom," he said.

After he had left, she removed her body from the cooled water. "Why didn't Jae-yong tell him to wait; or at least let me put on a robe?"

She kneaded her hair with the towel and then ran it over her face, chest, stomach and under her arms. She dressed and wiped the mirror with the towel, revealing a face much angrier than she had expected, then brushed her hair and, taking up her watch, strapped it around her wrist.

"6:35; dammit!" she said aloud.

She rushed out of the bathroom, and through the living room, just in time to hear Stanley say, "What's that smell?"

"It's Azra's dish," Jae-yong replied dryly. "It's burning."

"Burning," she thought. What was "burning," "screwing," "working," "driving," "bathing," and all the other functions? Was it the same as having "hair," "lips," "breasts," and "feet"? If it was her who was burning, would he also say, "She is burning," without lifting his eyes?

"We can eat now," she said, when the table was finally set.

Stanley approached with uncertainty, glancing back at Jae-yong.

"You don't have to eat it," he told Stanley.

He, Stanley, is a conduit, she felt. I am snow, she knew, falling on dark and empty streets; and I will build up, until I kill the sound of your steps   *the laughter stopped   cracked skin   numb. tracing. spheres*

Outside it was chilly. She had been in a hurry, forgotten her jacket, and now wondered if she would ever see it again.

She walked along the length of the platform, and then beyond, into the dark. To her right the new city jail rose up. She could see men, wearing orange jumpsuits, pace back and forth before the windows. The tracks gleamed and the smell of aged tar penetrated her. She walked with arms crossed over her chest and looked to her left, at a field of weeds, beyond which sat a row of warehouses, fenced in with barbed wire.

Walking to the edge of darkness, her feet patted the asphalt, lips sat one atop the other and eyes clouded. Light refracted from the tears, creating scintillas over

the bleak railyard. She turned. Branches, she wanted, a
blanket *rain   can't be   without that they were there
and flew   can't be   not be just want felt knew believed
disappearing into the clouds or darkness or what is it when
no longer feel   no longer know say if I am a jar full of
water and you are water and me the jar if you spill what
am I if you spill if spill pour in me pour in me my subtle
body   (absence)   in me but don't break it the jar me
pour me pour me   don't break the   can't be   because to
do it will hurt why am I crying be happy be happy   am*

The lives were only lives by name, just as the railroad
spikes were, in truth, metal, shaped to be driven with
a hammer.

62.

Sometimes I wish I could block out this . . . reality, be ignorant and therefore happy—in an animal way. But no, me . . . like a man with his hamstrings cut pulls himself along by his hands, eardrums bursting— roaring klaxons, eyes pricked with fine needles. . . . My karma I suppose . . .

I knew Giancarlo through a friend of mine, Claude Réjane, who lived on the Upper East Side. I would ride through subterranean passages, beneath the City, the 4 or 5 train, meditating on suburban darkness, on those arteries of Modern Civilization collapsing like the veins of a junkie.

Claude took me over to his sister's loft on the Lower West Side . . . giant, rambling, taking up much of the top floor of a building on the corner of Canal and West Broadway. . . . The walls were painted black and windows masked over with red rice paper. The place was hardly furnished, there were no chairs, only zafus, nylon cobwebs splayed in the corners, perverse German prints were pinned to the walls. A mannequin was propped against a lamp, her private parts smeared with green wax, dirty honeycomb protruding from her punctured eye sockets. The home of a poseur, I thought.

She was not at home . . . Claude had a key. . . . He started purring like a feline. I had the unsettling suspicion that he had brought me there to seduce me, fulfill his jaundiced fantasies.

He began chopping up cocaine. We filled our noses with numbness and he left and she and Giancarlo came in. I must say that my initial reaction was one of consummate disgust. . . . Beautiful, yes . . . of that there was no doubt. But she resembled Claude . . . had the same thick, sensual lips, the same mannerisms. It was as if I were witnessing the *phantom* of an attractive woman. . . . I thought she looked familiar, but at the time I merely attributed this to her resemblance to Claude. . . . It was only months later that I equated her with Geeta Greyhorse. If I had realized this from the get-go I undoubtedly would have been more discreet in my investigations, I would have had some inkling at least that the people I was dealing with were powerful figures in the clandestine world of depravity.

They seemed not at all surprised to find me there, I was treated as an old friend. Undoubtedly Claude had been delivering reports.

Giancarlo immediately sat down next to me and scoured the mirror with his nose, snorting like bull. Setting his wild, blood-webbed eyes on me, he asked to tell my fortune. They had me toss a handful of salt onto a plate. . . . Aeluromancy. . . . He let his tongue roll along, pick up speed, gain frenetic strength and volume. . . . What they told me . . .

In the months that followed he made many such ominous predictions; he read my shadow, the entrails of a fish bought in Chinatown, a red-hot iron, a bowl of cornmeal, a balanced hatchet. . . . They would entice me into smoking hashish and drinking baijiu with them. As I became more intoxicated Giancarlo would unveil before me strange, cryptic magazines, depicting naked old women, asexuals, and people with disfigured genitals. . . . He would laugh sadistically, winking at me like a goat, a disgusting satyr. . . .

. . . vermin running across the dark street, shapes, spies, hunched in corners, shadows shifting in alleyways.

I listened and watched, looked for camouflaged meaning in all his actions, his words. As zoologists study the feces of animals, trying to pry loose their nocturnal secrets, so I investigated . . . the trash in his bathroom, the contents of her medicine cabinet . . . I had no fear of handling those incarnadined feminine hygiene products—for I had profound hopes that they would lead me closer to the Truth. After my investigations I would flush the unused toilet and come out buttoning up my pants. . . . I had the awful feeling that he suspected my intentions. It was likely that he did away with the evidence in some highly sophisticated manner. Or else it was so blatant that I didn't see. . . . The real problem was that I had no clear idea what to look for. It might have been as small as a mustard seed . . . as large as an elephant.

There were three rusty razor blades in their medicine cabinet. I took one and hid it in my wallet—between my driver's license and ATM card. I had every intention, upon getting home, of examining the blade in detail—I would use the magnifying glass from my Oxford English Dictionary—search for suspicious traces—particles of hair, of diaper, of I knew not what . . .

I looked in my wallet. Gone! I tore it apart frantically. There was not a trace. "It might have dropped out," I told myself. I had taken the 6 train from Canal to 14th St. I walked to the 14th St. station scanning the ground the entire way. It was dark so I had to be careful, meticulous. On getting to the 14th St. station I boarded the 6. I got off at Canal and traced my steps back to West Broadway (once more searching the ground). There was no trace. I ran back to the subway station and (again) boarded the 6 (going uptown). I walked from car to car my eyes glued to the ground, the seats, the vacuous eyes of the passengers. . . . A subway attendant sat placidly in one of the cars. I asked him if he had found anything. He denied it. There was something unnatural about his manner. By the time we reached 42nd St. I had explored the length of the train. But how many trains were there on the 6 line? Twelve, fifteen? . . . I crossed the tracks and waited for the downtown train. . . . I spent the whole of that night riding the 6. Downtown. Uptown. From Brooklyn Bridge-City Hall to Pelham Bay Park.

Though I was discouraged I had no intention of giving up the struggle.

At home I secretly studied the Geeta Greyhorse films. . . . I bought the entire series. . . . During that period of my investigations I would awake in the morning my body and face marked by scratches, claw marks. . . . An ugly shopkeeper, a suet belly, his black hair salted with dandruff, finds that he repulses customers. . . . He hires an attractive girl, places her behind the counter . . .

While I was rewinding *Housewife,* the letters appeared. My flesh frosted, goose bumps like nipples, nipples like chestnuts. . . . Everything assumed an immense clarity. . . .

64.

The shafts of the sun began to pierce the window. He looked through the glare and made out dust rising from the drive below.

He watched as the tires turned up the last phase of the drive and then, in a burst of dust, braked to a halt. . . . The driver rolled out of the cab, hitched up his pants, and approached the door.

"Leaena," Jae-yong shouts with gentle sound. A person possibly wants the sound, but knows the stubborn compression molding them is useless. Jae-yong considers standing, but Samir does not have the invitation to enter his trouble. This person lives in the social kindness equator following certain distance, quite closely grasped the familiar extreme.

Leaena now appeared. Jae-yong requested that she boil water for tea. Samir, eyeing the woman's haunches; Jae-yong twisted his mouth into a grimace and told him to be seated.

The conversation turned, by design of the host, to alchemy.

"I have read all of Bumusa-Juba's work, in the original Arabic . . . practically know by heart Edward Kelly, *The Theatre of Terrestrial Astronomy* . . . Elias Ashmole, Simon Forman, John Dee . . . *De Heptarchia Mystica* . . ."

"It is not that this does not interest me," Jae-yong commented, removing a Turkish oval from his cigarette case and lighting it, "but that sort of vulgar alchemy I don't consider to be of ultimate consequence. We don't really need another Albertus Magnus to create a man or golem of brass—these days scientists, with their genetic manipulation and nanotechnology, far outdo the necromancers of old who dabbled in feeble magic. . . . And as for the other sort, men such as Nicholas Flamel, those who spent their precious time turning minute amounts of mercury into silver and gold. It seems to me that to draw a standard paycheque would prove more profitable."

"Excuse my saying this, Jae-yong," Samir said condescendingly, through curling lips, "but I do not believe you really understand what alchemy is all about. Turning mercury into gold is pure symbolism; it is not meant to be taken in the literal sense. I strongly suggest you read Ko Hung; that way you might have a little comprehension of the subject."

Just then Leaena walked in carrying a large lacquer tray on which were set a Yixing pot, a sealed container, and a few other items. Jae-yong arose from his seat, walked to the glass cabinet in which his pottery collection was kept, and removed two of the four Ming dynasty porcelain tea cups which were kept therein:

brightly-colored, from Jingdezhen. Removing the taut and glossy Lanxi Maufeng leaves, each single one attached to a delightful bud, he rinsed them with water from the pot, and then proceeded to make the beverage, doing his best to live up to Lu Yu's criteria for the proper infusion.

Jae-yong lifted the cup or aromatic liquid to his lips and took a sip, letting the slight astringency run over his tongue and glide down his throat.

"The truth is," he said, "that I am more than familiar with the Taoist authors. I suppose that is what I meant when I said alchemy: Something spiritual, or metaphysical, in order to transmute the dross of this world around me into gold: For, truly, you know, I see little that is beautiful about the current state of man. It—They—We, seem to fancy ourselves apart from the animal kingdom, the layerings of earth and stone, the bursting forth of foliage. Some indeed might rise above the status quo, the four-footed, the vegetable and mineral—those Artists, those Saints: that extreme minority whose works and deeds, whose examples whisper of the divine: a Gauguin, a Śāriputra, a Schnitzler—but the vast—and I do mean vast—the vast majority are nothing more than grim natural phenomena. Not beautiful phenomena. No; it, they or we are no roses, but more or less resemble belly-crawling reptiles. Truly there is little that is beautiful about the current state of . . . things."

"Man may not be as beautiful as a flower or star, but he is far more amusing."

jawless fish swims through thick sauce
silent sponge becomes screeching bat
Cro-Magnon man has become indolent
chest bouncing like a slaughterhouse
think of segmented worms and jellyfish
gold dust flutters around him
his tights revealing prominent hips

"More tea?" Jae-yong murmured, lifting up the Yixing pot.

He poured a second helping of the light, fragrant liquid into Samir's cup, and then filled his own, setting down the pot and taking up the smaller, slightly steaming vessel between three fingers.

[Maslamati ibn Ahmad al-Majriti, if he wanted to speak of alchemistry, the *Ghâyat al-Hakîm fî'l-sihr*; he had a delightful old Spanish edition of the text, *El fin del sabio y el mejor de los dos medios para avanzar*; and then he recalled his own exploits into natural magic (vague as a hallucination, plastic and fleeting) he had tried Della Porta's recipe for nice hair bruising marshmallow roots with pigs fat and boiling it with wine, cumin, mastic and egg yolks and anointing his own head and then with the fat of a horse's neck and a river eel dissolved in oil.]

65.

"Are you crazy?" Jae-yong shouted. "Dog of the law in us at the dawn of the eastern sky. But the spirit of the people fled to the mountains. There are also a few rocks leisurely in order to pursue her eyelids to us that the weakness of us are not so easy to find."

It wasn't hard for him to get me into his line of thinking and I acquiesced without argument I told Jae-yong I needed to rest we moved on through the shadows gurgling rivers and small creeks that tinkled branches brushing up against my face or slapping me on my shoulder like they were alive
a head propped
sharp steel
weight;
and imbecility
of rope
swinging legs
of lynches;
skin hung
in frightening wads
tortured mass

blossoms of spring
a curly golden wig
some ancient headdress found in the attic
once worn by a thin and peevish duke who had his
face ceaselessly powdered
portraits that as yet have been left unpainted.

66.

Mother, how I long to plant a crocus in your hair.

Were you jealous of those boys? I can assure you they meant nothing to me, beyond a little laughter and a tear. Yes, I know that you want me to have friends ever-lasting, and in the bottom of your heart realize who I am. But you I will keep for my own, my hidden gem, and observe your luster behind locked doors.

Do you know how much I love the old family photo albums? You have always been right in calling me sentimental. To live in the smiles of long ago is a beautiful thing.

The picture of you in your bathing suit at Lake Sumner has always inflamed my imagination in ways best left unsaid. It is so true that the styles of swimwear have only changed for the worse. I am old-fashioned and believe that to wear a one-piece would be charming.

And do you remember our trip to Muscle Shoals? What a hot summer it was. I recall vividly how impressed you were with Wilson Dam. It makes me sad to know, that the photos of that trip are mostly of me, and not of you—If there is an again, I will take all the pictures and let you pose.

There is another thing I have always wished to tell you: I am enchanted by women primarily when they eat fruit—strawberries, bananas and, of course, the plum. This is one action that us fellows will eternally be put to shame in. I wish it were otherwise, but, Mother, as you have often said, we live in a not quite perfect world.

67.

He had seen her vulva. Years later, she would go mad, lips torn, breasts lacerated.

Sandwich of hips, loaf of belly.

Ghosts that inhabited gnarled, dried-up tree trunks, mounds and abandoned shacks. Somewhere in the midnight of his mind a subterranean vendetta was being fulfilled. There are moods that linger on unseen; smell them faintly those secrets.

His mind retained those visions of the past, sexual embraces, dinners, tender moments, keeping them as if for eternity. Like a cloud he could see her naked body, legs spread, something transparent within him. But she had. She had run from him,
she had been lonely,
looking into the cool of his eyes,
his shallow affection.

More uxorious experience *smut. lust. flesh.* and tastes. Immortality, not disappearing to nothing, deep and dreamless.

His five senses all hunger after contact, external impressions. They long for sweetness, softness and beauty.

68.

A PARK. EXTERIOR. DAY.
Samir is walking through a park. He walks by a young man sitting on a park bench. It is Agustín, an old acquaintance.

AGUSTÍN: Samir! Don't you remember me? It's Agustín!

SAMIR: Yes, I remember you. [*Leaving.*]

AGUSTÍN: What's the hurry? Sit and speak.

SAMIR: No, I have to, um . . . be somewhere.

AGUSTÍN: Everyone has to . . . be somewhere; [*then in a low voice flashing a little baggy in the palm of his hand*] but don't you got the fever for the flavor?

DISSOLVE TO: THE BASEMENT OF MRS. CHENG'S. NIGHT.
Stanley has set himself up an art studio in Mrs. Cheng's basement. We see him painting a canvas. The painting is

unclear, but what we briefly glimpse is animalistic, geni-
tal, sensual. Mrs. Cheng calls to him from the top of the
stairs.

MRS. CHENG: Come on up now, Stanley. You must
get to bed. It's getting late.

STANLEY: Okay, I'll be up in a minute!

SHOT OF STANLEY WALKING DOWN THE
HALLWAY TO HIS BEDROOM.
He looks tired. He passes by Joe the Sky's room. The door is
open. He looks in.

SHOT OF JOE THE SKY'S ROOM FROM
STANLEY'S POV.
Joe the Sky is lying in bed, his face drawn and sickly. His
breathing is slow and labored.

MRS. CHENG [*her voice coming from off screen—she is*
behind Stanley]: Come on now and get yourself to
bed, Stanley!

TWO-SHOT OF STANLEY AND MRS. CHENG.
They are standing in the doorway.

MRS. CHENG: Don't worry about Joe, he'll be fine.
He just needs to be left alone. You just need to sleep
and leave him tranquil. He will be all right.

[*Exit Stanley. Mrs. Cheng cuts off the light and exits, clos-*
ing the door behind her.]

216

69.

The dining room of the Hotel Electra Palace was almost empty. It was off-season.

Yves Hermite sat back in his chair, eyes gazing blankly out the window, from time to time stretching his hand forward, wrapping his fingers around the glass of iced Drambuie before him, pulling it up to his sensual lips and taking a sip.

"Yes, not much to do in this town at this time of year," the waiter said. "Not for your type."

"My type?"

"Yes. Someone so . . . sophisticated."

"And what gives you the idea—that I am . . . sophisticated?"

The waiter made an indefinite, somewhat unctuous gesture with his hand. "I have worked in hotels almost my whole life," he said. "I can sum a man up in an instant."

"So?"

"So?"

"The game . . . tell me . . ."

"Well, for your type—the type who really knows something about . . ."

"Go on."

"Well, for your type the thing to do might be . . . to pay a visit to . . . the Azalea House."

"Flowers?"

"Naturally."

"I'm interested."

The waiter scribbled down an address on a piece of paper and slipped it to Yves Hermite, and Yves, in response, slipped him a banknote of reasonable denomination.

"Ask for . . . Pantea," the waiter murmured, and then stalked off.

Women were lined up, along the walls, one missing a leg, another an arm—everyone at least a hand, or a foot, or several fingers. Indeed, this was a temple for the devotees of Coyolxauhqui, the place where those fellows who stand staring at the Venus de Milo as they twirl their moustaches or fondle their canes go to . . . well . . .

Their features indistinct in the dim light, a few of these men sat off in corners, chatting in low tones with some of the ladies.

An immense woman wearing a satin and chiffon layer gown, burgundy in color, approached Yves. She asked him, in a strangely child-like voice, if anything he saw appealed to him.

"Is Pantea here," he asked.

The proprietress winked at him and motioned for him to follower her.

The creature sat there, a ball of flesh dripping with lace—armless, legless—a limbless and most attractive mate for any experienced bon vivant.

218

70.

I claw at the wall with my hands, hoping to tear away the particles, but I only succeed in breaking my nails, scraping raw the flesh of my fingers. Tears roll down my dry cheeks.

When I stop speaking the being on the other end begins. Even though I cannot really make out the words, this is a form of communication. Basic, primitive no doubt, but through the very vehemence of articulation it is both deep and meaningful.

. . . For I seem to recall, out of the depths of my existence, reading like some cacographic scripture, jointly ambiguous and untranslatable, that such a thing is possible, or at least is reputed to be.

My eyes close in exhaustion. . . . I am dreaming . . .

The nearer I get the more difficult it is to remain calm.

71.

Jae-yong sat by the drawing-room window, a cigarette burning in his fingers, a glass of brandy set by his side. The room was dark and outside the lawn silvery from the glow of a very full moon. He stroked his cheek and felt the slightest stubble of whiskers; he ran a thumb over his lips and felt their soft misery. Continuous contact with Yves Hermite had made him bitter and hateful. Indeed, many times he had been tempted to waylay him in the night with a stiletto, or poison his food with something deadly, or yet commit some crude act of butchery, club out his brains, strangle him with a thin cord.

He pressed the butt of his cigarette into the ashtray, and then drained off the liquor from his glass. Having risen to his feet, he made his way silently up the stairs and then, at the top, veered off to his own quarters. Yet, before he had moved many steps, he heard the sound of a door open behind him, and then whispers. He stood against the wall, turned and watched, listened. A soft, light giggle came to his ears, followed by the tenor of a spank, a smack and a variety of hiss.

watering herbs with sewage.

EXTERIOR. SEVERAL SHOTS OF JAE-YONG WALKING ALONG VARIOUS STREETS.

INTERIOR. THE CAFE WHERE AZRA IS SUP-POSED TO MEET JAE-YONG.
Azra sits at a table by herself trying to read Genitality in the Theory and Therapy of Neurosis *in the original German. It's obvious she can't concentrate. She keeps looking up expectantly. She sees Jae-yong from a distance and waves. Jae-yong approaches, removing his sunglasses.*

AZRA: Hello. I wasn't sure you would make it.

JAE-YONG: Well, I did.

AZRA: Yes, but where is it? Did you bring it?

JAE-YONG: No, I can't bring it into a place like this. It's too primitive to be grasped in this environment. I thought . . . we could go . . . if you were still interested . . .

AZRA [*looking slightly perplexed*]: Yes, I'm interested . . .

JAE-YONG: Well, I could say . . . but I would be lying . . . it's not . . . so why be formal . . . ?

[*Azra looks uncertain.*]

JAE-YONG: Don't worry.

AZRA [*laughing*]: All right.

CLOSE-UP OF AZRA'S BODY FROM JAE-YONG'S POV.

72.

As manners dictated that I could not so soon withdraw, I many times filled my mouth with brandy, determining that it might help forge my tastes in the model of my host's. Though this did not prove to be entirely the case, I can say that the beverage did help the hour to pass by easily enough. The jester, after giving ample evidence of his knowledge of low lyrics, as well as demonstrating his ability to somersault on the rug, withdrew, and I took the opportunity to plead exhaustion and beg leave to retire.

"By all means," said the Duke. "My apologies for keeping you away for so long from the rest which you must be so much in need of, and the bed which I have not the slightest doubts you will find to your satisfaction."

My body was tired from travel and my mind heavy from drink when I lay myself down, extinguishing the candle at my side with a single sighing breath. I thought not on the proceedings of the evening, nor on the strange locale in which I found myself, instead letting my mind drift off along a sea of fantastic dreams, only to be lay into the port of a startling awakening.

"Don't cry out so, it's only me," the voice said in German.

I could see the glint of her teeth, and their inward curve, by the glow a thin taper she held in her hand. She was atop me, her white locks snaking over shoulders and breasts, which were of alarming proportion and possessed all the boldness of line a woman of her years could very well desire. Still under the heat of wine, such a nocturnal adventure was not unwelcome to me, and I let her know as much in rambling words.

"Quiet," she hissed and then, setting the taper aside, my youth picked fruit, palm whipping offered freakishly spices was such a laugh, my joy, not against her craving.

"I'm not heavy to carry," she muttered.

A throaty sound; flying hair.

She gave her orders.

I complied, seizing the dilated objects and applying what pressure my waning strength permitted. She bayed with lupine avidity and proceeded to enact a series of paroxysms that made me fear for my very safety, advancing her weight with such vigor and insistence as might have crushed a man of lesser build. A shrill, disembodied cry rang out and then a whimpering, not unlike that of a dying animal. I felt my spine, dry and shrunken, tremble along my back.

73.

Yves Hermite looked out the window of the cab and saw buildings, and a few other things which were not buildings called trees. He felt something within him but did not analyze it. He leaned his head back and closed his eyes and imagined the air above and birds in the air. He thought of himself as a bird, having sex with other birds, mounting them, flapping his wings.

The cab let him off on Third Avenue and he went in the building.

The guard at the front desk spoke to him.

"Hello," Yves Hermite said, "I'm looking for suite number 810."

"Elevator. Eighth floor. Take a right."

In suite 810, Rusty Maddox was at the reception desk leafing through Lonely Planet's *India: a travel survival kit.*

"Is Mr. Harvey Shannon in?" Yves Hermite asked.

"Do you have an appointment?"

"It is about the manuscript."

"The manuscript?"

"You've read it?"

"I'm not . . ."

"That's his door?"

"Yes, but without an app——"

Yves Hermite had already turned and was at the door, thrusting it open.

74.

INTERIOR. MAURICE AND ALEX'S APART-
MENT. MORNING.
*Maurice sits on the couch reading a paper. We can vaguely
hear the argument of Jae-yong and Azra going on next-door.
Alex enters from the kitchen wearing an apron and carrying
a spatula.*

ALEX: Can you hear them next-door? Just terrible! All
   that arguing just ruins the morning.

MAURICE [*looking up*]: Couples argue, Alex.

ALEX: Well, from in here you can't hear as well, but the
   kitchen is certainly right next to their bedroom, and
   I'm telling you those walls are like tissue paper. I can
   make out every word they say. Oh! all that quarrelling
   just makes my blood run cold, or boil, or whatever
   it is that blood does when it gets extremely upset.
   I'm a little scared for the poor girl. I could hear him
   abusing her. Why must men act that way?

MAURICE: Oh, I'm sure she's fine. Just a lover's quarrel no doubt.

ALEX: Lovers without love!

MAURICE [*putting down the paper*]: Most people quarrel, Alex. What I wonder is what her boyfriend does for a living. He seems like an awfully strange man.

ALEX: I don't know. Maybe he's a gigolo or a poet or porn star or a pipe cleaner. What do I care? I just wish he would talk to his *lover* in a more domesticated tone.

CUT TO: SLOVENIA. A FIELD. DAY.
A woman sits shirtless in the field, with a lamb suckling at her breast. The woman has a dreamy look in her eyes. From somewhere in the distance, we hear the sound of a flute. It is playing Pietro Locatelli's "Flute Sonata Op.2 n°1".

75.

I thought I saw and heard other things as well, like faces and whispering voices in the dark. There were gloomy patches which crossed me and chilled me and the moonbeams flashed through the trees and danced like will-o-the-wisps.

When I awoke, light was pouring in through one of the windows as well as a few beams shafting down through holes in the roof. Jae-yong was snoring, a nearly empty bottle rolling on the floor next to him.

I lifted the bottle up and took a whiff. Dextromethorphan? Terpin hydrate? Ether? I wasn't sure. I set it down and took a look around, wondering where Jae-yong had acquired the substance.

There, on the other side of the room, was a whole stack of crates, each one full of bottles of it, neatly packed in mildewy hay. In one other corner there was a bottling apparatus and some general distilling gear.

- Dilated pupils
- Increased body temperature

- Increased heart rate
- Dry mouth
- Shakiness
- Sweating
- Numbness
- Weakness
- Nausea
- Panic
- Terror
- Despair
- Swift emotional changes
- Hallucinations
- Delusions

He was still there in the bed, his face turned against the wall. He growled and moved his shoulder. Then he was sitting up, his two eyes glaring at me.

"Hell," I said, "if the bear suffered a haven for hitching horses perform other aspect of the twelve."

I associate the word for it, but it helps, go ahead I add details to an already was.

Cricket is a public body squat on their black crows are playing with each other and this is set to warble fly to roost in the treetops frisking, he cawed.

I am inside the castle—could hear nearly agitation. I myself was ready for a start, some feel hungry belly wood strength, so I dig another strip of corn in my gender—were inside the hoof and muscle meal. He is a good deal looking ominous, slightly mad bull, like his face, his rosy wild eyes kind of like another bottle uncorking sitting there on my light dying in an old bed and the moonlight was me and looked up.

"Management of the water to eat the roots?" I asked, setting the food in my own bed.

"I do not figure out," he answered quietly. "I just think thirsty, but it does not appeal to me now. I think a lot of food."

I extracted a piece of my chin beef. Each of us, except my chewing sound, silence, sit him words that passed between us. I can without a male.

After I had swallowed the last morsel of what was set before me, I reached for my cup, but it was empty.

Outside it was pure night and the stars in the clear sky above twinkled like a diamond necklace. From over the hill a coyote let out its mournful bark and, as if in response, a great horned owl flew right in front of me, alighting on the branch of a dead tree.

The water was like a sheet of oil, the light of the rising moon glinting off it in shimmering patches. It gurgled gloomily.

I climbed back up the hill. We were there in the cradle of those ancient mountains.

I saw Jae-yong's black outline in one corner.

76.

In Ankara he sat in a hotel room for days together smoking the black Moroccan tar from a hookah, his eyes the pink of rare beef.

He regurgitated, on an open plain in Chihuahua, Mexico, mescaline in the form of peyote cactus. He was filled with a pleasant lightness, a sort of cerebral buoyancy. This amusing intoxication, however, rapidly transformed itself into a more serious manifestation. Jae-yong's body began to dissolve, until he was veritably unconscious of it; he felt as a soul unsheathed. A liquid and living bas-relief, skeletons and morbid beings, some simply feet with heads, others beaked and cloaked, bearing bloody weaponry, danced around fires upon which his own human kind turned on violent spits . . . "The worm that never dies, that which lies sleeping within us all, was made tangible and an external thing, and clothed with a garment of flesh," he thought, and trembled, quoting Arthur Machen. . . . Samir danced around the room, his ears elongated, a hideous, sardonic laugh burping forth from his organ of speech.

77.

"So I hope you liked that."

"I did."

They got in Samir's car and left the movie theater. He did not drive towards where Servilia lived.

"You don't mind if we go for a little ride now, do you?" he said.

He pulled off onto a dirt road and then pulled over to the side. Servilia felt very nervous. She looked out the window, at the immense darkness and profiles of trees against the night. She moved closer to him and he put his arms around her and held her.

It was a little after ten in the morning and Samir sat on the curb. He pulled a miniature of El Jimador tequila from his pocket, drank it in two separate swallows and then chased it with coffee from a Styrofoam cup.

When he got to the window he took the .38 snub-nosed revolver out of the paper bag and pointed it at the teller. She smiled at first and then, when she understood, became very frightened. She started unloading the money from her cash drawer. She was behind that Plexiglas window and would not have been hurt even if Samir had fired the gun, but apparently did not take this into consideration or did not trust her life to a transparent sheet.

CUT TO: ANCIENT ROME. THE GROVE OF SIMILIA. DAY.
Women, naked aside from crowns of grape-leaves, sport naked as they drink from enormous bowls of unmixed wine. They grab each other, kiss, push each other away, touch, and touch again.

GEETA GREYHORSE: Time it seems yet just a game . . . your voice, I hear it in my dreams, begging for the taste of my breasts. Crimson petals and cerise lusts, both make me cry . . . but coral-colored wine is what gives my mouth delight.

CUT TO: SHOT OF JAE-YONG, AZRA AND STANLEY SPEEDING DOWN THE HIGHWAY IN A CONVERTABLE CAR.

SHOT OF THEM AT THE BEACH.
They are lounging on towels in the sand. The beach is crowded. Jae-yong swims out into the ocean; we can see him in the distance. Azra and Stanley splash each other with water at the surf's edge. There is a collage of shots of various beach activities. In many of them Stanley is seen admiring Azra in her bikini as she innocently sports with him.

78.

MEDIUM TWO-SHOT OF AZRA AND JAE-YONG.

AZRA: We should take Stanley out more often.

[Jae-yong shrugs his shoulders.]

CUT TO: INTERIOR. THE LEGION OF HONOR. DAY.
We see Jae-yong and Azra guiding Stanley through the museum. They walk past an anthropoid coffin, then a secrétaire from 1763, then a sculpture by Benvenuto Cellini. They stop to admire a painting by Rembrandt. Azra and Stanley seem happy. Jae-yong's features are impenetrable.

CUT TO: INTERIOR. THE AQUARIUM. DAY.
Azra and Stanley are looking at fish, Azra pointing out various creatures of interest. We see sharks and eels. Jellyfish float mysteriously by. Giant tube worms and sea snails. Rainbows, blinking eyes, puckered mouths. A two-headed snake.

DISSOLVE TO: THE LIVING ROOM OF AZRA'S APARTMENT. MEDIUM-SHOT OF AZRA THROUGH THE BATHROOM DOOR. DAY.

Azra is taking a bubble-bath. The bathroom door is open so we can see her from the living room. She hears the door buzzer and hops out of the tub, wrapping a towel around her—briefly seen nudity.

AZRA [*to herself*]: Jae-yong must have forgotten his door key when he left.

[*She presses the door release button and then talks over the intercom.*]

AZRA: Okay, it's open.

[*She cracks open the front door and then goes back in the bathroom and gets in the tub. There is a pause and then we hear somebody walk in.*]

AZRA [*calling out*]: It's open; I'm in the tub! Did you have any luck? Did you find it? . . . Hello, is any-body there?

[*She looks up and sees Stanley standing in the bathroom door. There is a moment of awkwardness.*]

AZRA [*nervously*]: Oh! If you just wait in the living room I'll be out in a moment.

[*There is an uncomfortable pause during which Stanley just stands there, staring blankly. He then turns away and closes the door behind him.*]

CUT TO: AFRICA. DAY.
We see men ritualistically having sex with holes in the ground. A drumbeat thumps and we hear the sound of birds flapping their wings.

CUT BACK TO: THE LIVING ROOM OF AZRA'S APARTMENT.

AZRA: I'm sorry. I thought you were Jae-yong. I didn't mean to embarrass you.

[*A pause during which Stanley stares nervously at Azra.*]

AZRA [*uncomfortably*]: You see, he was going to look for it. Actually we have been looking for it for some time now. But I got tired of looking with him.

STANLEY [*in a barely audible voice*]: I . . . I'm looking too.

79.

I can hear something moving. Is it me, myself? No. I feel my legs, my arms. I am quite still. Yet certainly this is no hallucination.

I slowly, with the most pure concentration, crawl toward the bucket. I can hear him clawing around in there. I feel the bucket gently, silently with my fingertips, the body, the rim. I shove my hand in quickly, violently grabbing my tormentor.

Pain shoots through my hand, immediate and terrifying.

A continuous tapping echoes in my brain, undoubtedly a further method of driving sense from it.

I can distinctly hear it.

It vibrates through the wall.

I listen.

Who are you?

WHO ARE YOU?

WHO ARE YOU?

WHO ARE YOU? WHO ARE YOU? WHO ARE YOU? WHO ARE YOU? WHO ARE YOU? WHO ARE YOU? WHO ARE YOU? WHO ARE YOU? WHO ARE YOU? WHO ARE YOU?

80.

The bus jogged out the gate, the windows marked
with heads drowned silent by the noise of the engine.
It shifted down the two-lane road, an exhalation of
black refuse trailing out of the tail-pipe. Inside, the oc-
cupants hummed in monotonous and dull imbecility,
sometimes marked by a sudden upshot of intelligence
and even comprehension.

"They might not have let it go, but that doesn't
mean that they don't have it," Samir thought.

"I believe it is the season of the salmon run," the
man next to him said. "I have a safety pin in my pocket
which I will take and tie on a string which I will tie to
a stick. A willow stick which I will find by the bank of
the stream and strip of its extraneous branchings. I will
tie a medium-sized pebble to the string which will act
as a weight. I will bait the pin with a worm which I
will dig from the soil as the night crawlers I used in my
youth. Casting the line in the water which will ripple,
I will wait with patience for the fish which you and I,
friend, will eat for our lunch."

Samir nodded in agreement, or alliance; but it was
not agreement with the gaunt and gesticulating figure

next to him. The bond was with seasoned and compacted chaos. The logic of the masks was the logic of the onion skin, and the layers of seats and heads in front of him—the layers of diagnosis; bread crumb trail of reason; the wild hands continuing to emphasize the turgid flow of voice:

"The pin is in my pocket and it will not open. I wrapped three bands of tape around it so it will not open. The fire I will start with a match. The matches are in my shirt pocket, which, as you can see, is secured by a button. Should the button come undone the possibilities of friction would increase, and thereby combustion. Should this occur, my shirt front would burn up, and you too, friend, would catch fire. The pin is secured by tape, friend, so I believe the likelihood of it coming unclasped is small. It should not prick me. I will be very careful when I bait it with the day worm which I will dig from the soil."

81.

MRS. CHENG'S KITCHEN.

Coffee is brewing. Mrs. Cheng takes three pineapple buns out of the refrigerator. She pours herself a cup of coffee, adds sugar and cream, and sits down at the kitchen table. She starts to eat the pineapple buns while sipping at her coffee. There is a time lapse. The pineapple buns are gone, just a few crumbs left on the plate and she is draining away the last of her coffee. She looks at her watch, gets up, takes a plastic garbage bag out of a drawer and exits.

STANLEY'S ROOM.

Mrs. Cheng enters holding the plastic bag. She closes the door behind her and approaches Stanley.

CLOSE ONE SHOT OF STANLEY'S FACE.

He seems to scarcely be breathing.

MEDIUM TWO-SHOT OF MRS. CHENG AND STANLEY.

Mrs. Cheng looks intently at Stanley. She takes the plastic garbage bag and sticks his head in it. She takes some

*masking tape from her apron pocket and masks off the bag
around the neck.*

EXTREMELY CLOSE SHOT OF PLASTIC BAG.
*We see, written on the bag, the words, "**WARNING:**
TO AVOID DANGER OF SUFFOCATION, KEEP
THIS PLASTIC BAG AWAY FROM BABIES AND
CHILDREN. DO NOT USE THIS BAG IN CRIBS,
CARRIAGES, OR PLAYPENS."*

CLOSE TWO SHOT OF STANLEY AND MRS.
CHENG.
*The bag follows the rhythm of Stanley's breath, expanding
and contracting. He starts moving his head back and forth.
His arms spontaneously reach for the bag. Mrs. Cheng
grabs them and holds them down. She climbs on top of
him, straddling him. She covers his head with a pillow, sits
on it and keeps his arms tacked down with her knees. His
body struggles weakly and then becomes still.*

THE HALL. SHOT OF MRS. CHENG COMING
OUT OF STANLEY'S ROOM.
*She is coming out of Stanley's room, dragging his dead
body. She drags it over to a laundry chute and, with a
great deal of effort, manages to put it in.*

DOWNSTAIRS. THE LAUNDRY ROOM.
*She is pulling the body out of the laundry chute. It is
somewhat stuck. She manages to get it loose, cursing all
the while.*

MRS. CHENG'S BATHROOM.

Mrs. Cheng stands naked over Stanley's body which is in the bathtub. She has an old Chinese meat cleaver that is quite large. She bends over the body, disappearing off screen. Her arm is seen, brandishing the meat cleaver, rising and falling with brutal hacks, drops of blood being distributed on the white surfaces.

DISSOLVE TO: EXTREMELY CLOSE SHOT OF BATHTUB DRAIN.

Blood is filtering down the drain. The camera pans up to Mrs. Cheng taking a shower. We see her breasts. An hour or two has elapsed. She has disposed of the body and she is now washing the blood off of herself and out of the bathtub. She soaps her body.

MRS. CHENG'S BEDROOM.

There is a poorly done painting of plum blossoms on the wall. She has gotten out of the shower and sits nestled in her bed, in her nightgown, reading a book by Jane Austen.

82.

Do you remember, Mother, how we used to talk of what I would be? In my pajamas I snuggled close to you, and was soothed by the breath of your sweet mouth. How did you make your teeth so white, and lips so jungle-red? If I knew this, and other secrets, the love of orchids might last for longer than an hour.

In the fall we walked through the woods, me with my yellow suspenders, you with your broad straw hat. The mushrooms called to us, the boletus, the morel, and how attracted we were together, to those moist and conical caps. Do you know, it was you who first told me, that to eat such things could be deadly? But how we enjoyed the succulence of those that were safe and there. They were more than just a feast for the eyes.

And have I ever told you, that still I awake, from dreams of those days, and mushrooms?

Yes, it is true—I have far too many pairs of boots for a man who prefers to wear Oxfords. But you know, Mother, how much I adore the smell of leather and the grooming of the soldier. I would lean against the trunk of a tree and examine its roots, while you, with your little knife in hand, continued to sever the stems of the mushrooms we would later fry in butter.

83.

They would come and unbutton their shirts. I came in and saw her kneeling. I thought she was praying. I thought she was praying. They had hair on their chests and moustaches and I could see the red hair on his chest and I slept in the little bed in the closet

inside there were books, many books

let his lazy eyes rest on the bronze head of Lucius Caecilius Jocundus, the famous banker from Pompeii. It was an anonymous work. Praxilites, Lysippos, the sculptor to Alexander the Great

the *Apoximenos*, the young man scraping mud and sweat from his body before bathing

Bryaxis, Kanachos, Antenor, Kritos, Nesiotes, Hageladas and his brilliantly famous students who would change the way man looked at man for eternity: Phidias [praeter Iorem Olympium and also a beautiful bronze Amazon and an Athena of pure ivory et alterum colossicon nudum], Myron [pubem non emendatius fecisse, etc.] and Polyclitus with his many pupils: Argeios, Asopodoros, Aristeides, Phryon, Deinon, Athnodoros, and Demeas of Kleitor the bronze found in the sea off Marathon, one hand extended as if to pluck some delicate fruit

she was in the bathroom and I knocked and knocked and then the woman from upstairs heard me crying and yelling and came down and used a hairpin to open the door and I could see her head thrown back and her long and pure hair. I could see her arm and it was white and everything was red and I looked past her to the puddle

the vase painters: Lydos, Epiktetos, Xenophantos. The true painters: Parrhasius and his rival Zeuxis, Nicomachus, Polygnotus, Apelles and his friend Protogenes, the great colorist

84.

I remember as a child of twelve . . . I was playing with a friend of mine . . . down in the gully. . . . I noticed that he was staring at me, his face yellow with terror.

"You have a scorpion on your shoulder," he said, his lips flapping like wings.

The scorpion whispered in my ear, "Take your hands and tear out his hair . . . poke out his eyes . . . stuff his mouth full of sand . . . bury his body deep in the ground."

As daylight fled the paved streets, the filthy walls of buildings, I walked; my elbows knocked against by overgrown spermatozoa, women in tight black pants, legs thin and rigid as jail bars. . . . I slithered up Broadway . . . across Houston. Faces were plunged in darkness. . . . I suddenly realized that all these twelve million people were bodies walking around with huge bubbles on their shoulders. . . . A bundle sat at the door . . . wrapped in plastic . . . paper . . . I brought it inside . . . coagulated blood. . . . I took it outside and threw it in the trash.

Finally, courageously, I climbed the steps, my underarms perspiring. . . . Claudia answered the door. Her body was sheathed in a maize-colored dress, hair done up in a dense bun. Waves of fragrance rose from her.

She sunk her nails deep in my face . . . Giancarlo rushed in from some dark passage. . . . They forced me to the ground. I wept. I knelt at their feet.

. . . Yes, as a child a man accosted me. He asked me my name. My age . . . "Are you a good boy?" he asked.

"Yes," I said.

". . . and when you die?"

"I'll be a spirit. I'll go to heaven."

"And . . . you don't want . . . to kill . . . enjoy?" he queried . . . massaging himself. . . . He reached for me. . . . My young mind became scrambled . . . I quivered, ran, spat on the ground . . .

85.

Yves Hermite held a marijuana cigarette of incredible thinness between his nimble fingers.

"We had better go back in my bedroom to smoke this," he whispered. "I don't want my mother to catch us."

Uncertainly, Samir followed him to the bedroom.

The room was as neat and well-ordered as that of a hotel. The furnishing and decoration were conservative. There was a queen-size bed set squarely in the center, a dresser with mirror and a little desk off in the corner with an antique toy Pullman train car on it and a miniature of the Venus de Milo. On a shelf was arranged the complete works of Paul de Kock, in a twenty-five volume set. The aroma of Yves Hermite was even more pronounced in the room where he slept.

"Sit down next to me," he said, seating himself on the edge of the bed.

Samir set himself down by the man whose lips protruded, heart-shaped, and emitted a thin stream of smoke.

As Yves Hermite passed it to Samir with his right hand, he placed the left on the fellow's knee.

86.

She was very close.

It was orchids and birds of paradise. They were the wrong flowers.

The rounded heads sat on both sides. My shadow stretched behind me and aped me. There was a fizzle. The sound came suddenly. A spray of water slashed across my legs. The sprinkler system must have been on a timer. Everything is like that.

My feet squashed through the grass. I found where I had set that ridiculous bouquet. The pick sank into the soft earth. I took the shovel and could feel the strain on my arms as I tossed aside the clods. I took off my shirt and tossed it too aside. The gentle breeze touched my skin and I shivered. I scraped away the dirt and threw it over the edge of the hole. With my bare hands I cleared the surface.

With the edge of the shovel, and with initial difficulty, I pried it open. The nails screeched as they left the wood.

There was cloth which I felt and tore at. The moon, which had always been near, appeared over tops of the trees and let its light fall to the hole. I put my lips to hers and noticed the smell.

CUT TO: PENTECOST ISLAND, VANUATU. DAY.
The sound of chanting. With lianas tied to their ankles, young men who have refrained from sex dive from a large tower, headfirst. Women watch from below, nodding their heads in satisfaction.

CUT TO: SHOT OF EAGLES FIGHTING IN THE SNOW. DAY.
High in the mountains, two eagles fight majestically in the snow.

CUT TO: SINGAPORE. RED-LIGHT DISTRICT OF GEYLANG. NIGHT.
We see Cult members handing out literature describing the benefits of a sexual relationship with Jesus. Prostitutes in latex mini-skirts linger around smoking cigarettes while fidgety young men on dope lean against buildings, other cigarettes hanging like icicles from their mouths.

CULT MEMBER #1: Must live by faith alone . . .

CULT MEMBER #2: Excommunication will occur if you do not submit to the Love of Jesus . . .

CULT MEMBER #3: The body of the shepherd is wise . . .

87.

The Duke, his passions inflamed by the sights, called Miss Vronsky to him and, with an imperial wave of his hand, indicated his requirements. The woman, still displaying the same frosty equanimity which was her principal characteristic, proceeded to pray at his damnable temple, while he soused her with pejorative remarks, which flowed from betwixt his scarlet lips with bubbling ease.

"Rogero," Madame cried out. "My flanks! Apply that damnable crop to my flanks!"

The manikin acquiesced with glee, taking up the riding crop and with it swatting her haunches, an expression of unmitigated joy flowering on his features. With head thrown back and her inward turned teeth sparkling in the light, the Countess von Strobe labored, her own body suffering the paroxysms of one possessed hail tearing everything to shreds thunderings and tintinnabulations a shiver coursing up her back her legs enjoyed glittering romances she longed for adventure.

The Countess dismounted, leaving, to all appearances what seemed a corpse in her wake.

I looked toward the Duchess, who stood off to one side, a strange, demented smile playing upon her lips, but her gaze did not meet mine. I rejoiced that my presence thus far had been more or less ignored, but I soon was relieved of that consolation by the voice of the Duke, asking me if I would not join them in their filthy pleasures.

"Even were such sights as these apt to excite me," I responded, "there would be but little hope of me being able to function as a man should, for the ammunition of my ardor has already been well expended on your delightful mother."

"Have no fear on that score," the Duke laughed and instructed the soiled Miss Vronsky to fetch some potions and unguents from a nearby cabinet.

This she did with dignified haste, producing a decanter of greenish liquid and a box of some sort of foulsmelling balm. She filled the glass that had contained the brandy from the decanter and had me drink. I knew not if it was poison or otherwise, but at that moment valued my life at naught—for I was bound with seemingly insurmountable adversity to overcome if I were to ever breathe the air of freedom again, and, indeed, I believed my best hope was to comply with the perverse whims of the Duke, thereby possibly winning some share of his clemency; for my body was his to do as he pleased with; he could let me live or die as he wished. With strong, cold hands she applied the unguent. I had always been skeptical of such things, having heard from reliable sources that they never worked and were only purchased by fools and cuckolds desperate to try any measure to resume their matrimonial hold. In this case, however, I was undeceived, for if the amorous medicaments of Padova were ineffectual, those of the Duke were the very opposite, refurbishing the snake with an ample supply of venom and invigorating the man in me with a fresh stock of dash.

The Countess laughed with great mirth as she saw me thus, but I blushed not, for shyness has never been my nature. She came to me and, setting my ears and neck in the nest of her viper-like kisses, proceeded to untie my ropes. The Baroness was then directed by her husband to go to me, which she did. Our intercourse, however, proved not to be satisfactory entertainment for the spectators, because we performed it like man and woman I suppose, in a somewhat noble fashion, and not like beasts or demons, as the Duke and his mother undoubtedly wished. The latter came close and, pulling the Duchess from me, said to her, "You are indeed a spiritless woman. You go about the thing so mincingly, as if to do so makes it any less a damnation."

Forthwith she called Miss Vronsky over and ordered her to take the Duchess's place. The faithful servant complied without the least complaint, casting off her garments with hasty care and exposing a body well-designed, firm and of a whiteness I had never witnessed before. She applied this edifice of pallid flesh to my olive-complexioned figure with the same impenetrable deportment she must have put into all her duties, though by all means that cold gravity did not in the least detract from the skill or force with which she went about the process. It was apparent that if such a woman were but endowed with a heart that pumped warm blood through her veins she would have made the ideal mistress, for though lacking tenderness, she was an excellent bedfellow.

The Duke and his mother were both excited by the sight, their hands straying with narcissistic devotion over their own figures while their eyes drank in the spectacle before them. I, under the influence of the drugs, became caught up in the activity and felt a riotous need for achievement. The Duke cried out with bravado, complimenting me on my skills, and then, reaching a degree of heat he could no longer control, threw himself upon his own wife and began using her with the utmost brutality. The Countess, not wanting to be left alone, grabbed up little Rogero and took him to a corner, where she exploited him without mercy and he asked for none. The chamber, filled with raw strains of lust, would surely have presented an odd spectacle to any onlooker.

88.

YOU CROSSED THE FINISH LINE WITH YOUR
PENIS SHEATHED IN LITTLE SHORTS.

89.

Both the pick and shovel were slung over one shoulder. The night was clear and the almost full moon shone brightly. Crickets chirped, the sound seeming to ricochet from one ear to the other.

The gate was locked. I threw the pick and shovel over the wall, one at a time. The pick-axe landed, producing a non-resonating sound. The shovel must have hit stone; it rattled. I climbed over. It was easy and made me think of other walls that I had climbed.

Once inside, the trees blocked out the larger portion of moonlight. There were plants and I felt them with my hands, their smooth and serrated tongues. I saw their jagged profiles.

I could hear the wind, which was gentle, brush through the leaves.

I drew a breath, sighed, looked around and got my bearings. I picked up the gear and walked down the path, gravel crunching beneath my feet.

I thought of her and her beauty. I buried my head in her hair and smelled its fragrance, felt it, and how soft it was. To open my eyes and be next to her was comforting.

I smelled the eucalyptus. The obelisks and monuments stood as the black skyline of a dead city. In the distance I heard a car speed by. It was probably a drunk making his way home at that late hour. Who did he have waiting for him? I stood still and listened. The sound of the motor receded into the night. There was nothing and I felt alone.

As I walked, the pick-axe and shovel scraped against each other. I put one over each shoulder. I separated them so that they would be quiet. The path went from the big trees into the newer section. It was flooded with moonlight. The grass looked very white, as if it had been covered with a coat of snow. Far off to my left I could make out the caretaker's cottage. A small green truck was parked in front.

I turned right and walked along the edge of the older section, the moon casting my shadow into the darkness. I felt that it offered me protection and I was satisfied to be blended into the obscurity. The trees were older than I was. They would shield me.

90.

"What seems to be the problem?" he said. He was scratching and talking.

I scratched too; I'm not a bird, but I scratched too. They were falling and I was scratching. I was fire. I scratched because I was fire.

It was hot flames and I fell on the floor. It tickled me down there and then moved up in my belly and sung in my throat. She came down and held me. I rolled. It was hot in me and she cried. I rolled.

He was scratching himself.

I rolled.

She held and petted me. We crossed the yard and I heard the leaves. I was a fish's heart. The window was open and my hair moving, knowing it *filling up around me. Blood.*

And I saw the blue flames above and heard it whisper. It whispered *torment and blisters and all the fierce affliction.* They took me out and brought me inside and I felt it.

His voice brought it on. It whispered and I whispered and some looked. They looked.

He started rubbing himself on the chair.

My nose cut off and burnt to ashes.

I could hear his feet and he was dancing. His arms were shaking. He put his hands on me. He put them on my head.

Killing in the river of blood.

I spat red guts. I was a fish's heart.

91.

Rusty Maddox lay on the bed in his room at the Hotel Royal International. Sweat was apparent on his face, his shirt was saturated, he could feel it dank on his legs. A water cooler blew the foul street air toward him, a tepid bath of vapor.

He had arrived in New Delhi the day before, but had hardly set foot outside his lodging. It seemed, from the moment he had descended from the plane, as if he were under the effects of a tropical fever, a strange malaise.

Sitting up, he drank warm bottled water, then arose and walked into the hall, down the steps and into the lobby. The desk clerk looked up, scrutinized Rusty's flushed face, and nodded. A Russian woman, tremendous, haggled over the black market exchange rate with the proprietor of the establishment.

On the street he was struck by the infamous malodor of the Main Bazaar; ruinous, a frappé of sulfur and goat.

With weak and swerving steps he went. Flies landed on him, which he nervously shooed away. Undoubtedly disease clung to their pulvilli, were distributed on one's skin by the proboscis, the hairy and lubricated labellum. He was in the habitat of their victims: near-naked boys; a fellow in tattered breeches, barefoot, his mouth encrusted with a white residue; a fat man with a white beard and turban coughing terribly; women, loose flesh and swollen tongues; beggars, legless, derelict; featherweight octogenarians bent under life-crushing loads, exotic, curious bundles; a boy with enormous, elephantine feet flopped alongside him. . . . Misery! . . . From every direction he was assaulted with unpleasant sights, touted for handouts, asked inexplicable, unanswerable questions, grinned at, frowned upon.

The ground trembled beneath his feet, the sky was adjusted at an odd angle, a dizzying tilt. He would have liked to have leaned against something, but every wall appeared as a barrier of malicious microbes. So many eyes were following him.

"Back to the hotel. . . . The first plane to the U.S.A. . . ." he told himself, turning, retreating.

92.

Rusty retired to the roof where he was informed that food was served. There were a few plastic tables with lawn chairs around them. A pile of canine defecation sat blackened in one corner.

The Hotel Royal International.

No other guests were in sight. The sky was overcast and the humidity seemed to increase.

He ordered a large bottle of Indian beer and a few chapatis. His stomach hardly seemed fit for anything more strenuous, yet he knew that he needed to ingest something.

He drank the beer from the bottle, disdaining the glass set before him, not trusting it to his lips. The liquid felt incredibly refreshing as it flowed down his throat, faintly bitter, slightly sweet, if not ice-cold, certainly cool, pleasantly cool. He held the bottle up to his forehead, rolled it across his heated brow. The newly acquired calm grew more pervasive as he looked out over the city.

The young man, who acted jointly as waiter, bell-hop, and room service, brought out a plate of chapatis. He smiled, a pleasant creek, setting them down.

"Here you are, sir."

He could not have been more than twenty. A dark film filamented above his upper lip. His eyes were soft.

"What country?" he asked.

Rusty told him.

The waiter, who introduced himself as Cyrus, said that an uncle of his worked in a restaurant in New York City, on Second Avenue. Somehow this fact, or fiction, made Rusty Maddox feel more comfortable with the young man. He himself lived in New York, in Queens, and worked in Manhattan, at the Shannon Agency.

Vacation.

Maybe write some poems.

He still had . . . hopes . . .

He experienced the beer, lightening the load of his brain. . . . While eating the Indian bread, he unburdened himself to this other human being, quite happy to hear his own vocal apparatus functioning in such perfect order. Cyrus listened, or at least stood there, his eyes meeting the other's, in a ciphering sort of way.

"What do you need?" the young man suddenly interrupted. "I can help you out. . . . You need . . . a good woman? . . . Nice boy? . . . The opium? . . . Heroin? . . . Marijuana . . . hashish . . . ?"

Thoughts, fractions of visions, quickly and fancifully passed through Rusty's mind—an Indian prostitute would be something, honey-skinned, melon-breasted, trained from infanthood to the one hundred and eight

arts of love, the intricate science of carnal pleasure—
but of course that was out of the question; these
women must harbor a veritable catalogue of diseases;
one would pay dearly for that hour of bliss, that instant
of satisfaction. . . . A boy? . . . No. . . . But maybe a few
joints . . . or some hashish . . .

93.

I have been told that I'm sensitive and I believe it. She helped me down off the curb and then held my elbow as we crossed the street, and then back up the curb on the other side. My face was on fire and I could feel that there was me and then there was her and that I was different and separate from her and it did not feel good. But when I looked away, I could see my feet and how they moved along the sidewalk and I could hear the sound as they did, like the wind and regular and the legs of my pants rubbed together and it was wonderful.

I was lagging behind. The real problem though was not so much walking faster than the rest of them, for I knew I could do that much, but was more trying to find an opportunity to pass them. I would have liked to have gone on and walk on the grass. I could see the light reflecting off his head and feel the warmth on my cheeks and beneath my arms. That is when I knew that we were getting close and something welled up inside me and made me anxious like I was too much for my feet and my knees to take.

94.

On his bed he sat, legs crossed, shirt removed. Cyrus had brought him room service tea, a cube of black dough, and a paper bag with cigarette papers and the dried brownish flowers. Rusty heavily sugared the tea, using the honey-colored crystals, the raw sweetener. He lit the cylinder, contrived carefully, a mixture, marveling how, earlier, he had been so prone to panic, absurdly paranoid, shut off from the local color.

Blue-gray coils of smoke rose up, scattered as they came in line with the swamp cooler, its thick, humid breeze. The tea, hotter than air, was pleasant, served in a glass that clicked against his teeth as he drank. He expected powerful results from the drug that burned between his fingers, the cherry that smoldered in the semi-darkness of the room. For a brief span, a matter of seconds, his suspicions re-awakened, the compulsion for self-protection, instinctive distrust of foreign lands, tropical climates, worshippers of strange gods. Then he experienced a cerebral injunction, a mellow dullness of the frontal lobe, a gathering numbness. He wet the orifice that marred his face with the liquid, tanned with milk. An odor, reminiscent of a stable, filled the room. He lay on his side, head propped up by a hand connected to a crooked arm.

At first the creatures on the ceiling were just dots and lines. Of course blossoms opened. . . . It seemed only natural. . . . They had wide, gaping mouths on their bellies, eyes on the palms of their hands; so many hands. One had the head of a rooster, another the arms of a squid. Some were endowed with strange, thin, pendulous breasts that hung to their knees, the nipples forked like a snake's tongue. Others were fat, with coal-blue skin, plumes of poppy-red hair that flowed slowly and gently as seaweed underwater. . . . In a circle they, the creatures, moved, a spiral, gesturing, genuflecting primitively. . . . It did seem that one smiling, pleasant creek face was familiar. . . . Rusty felt like calling out, to Cyrus. And then it came out of his throat, that thing, but the breathing was so difficult.

95.

A dull and continuous throb. His stomach and genitals ached. There was a disgusting and medicinal essence . . . And the room? . . . No, he did not recognize it. . . . A curtain covered the window, puffed out by a slight breeze, its green material tingeing the light. . . . But that dull, obnoxious pain, from between his legs. . . . He felt for his genitals. . . . Where? . . . Horrified, he lifted his hand before his eyes, the fingers covered with a brownish-red muck.

96.

She felt Samir's face, like a blind woman, his cheek-bones, down his face to his neck, over where there was not a chin. She did not know whether she was driven by middle-aged woman's lust or despair and did not care what was outside the darkness, what was outside the intoxication produced partly by alcohol mostly by what she had in her hand.

He woke up and looked over at the woman next to him. The light from the porch came in through the window and he could see her face, worn and sad. He got out of bed and put his pants on, reached over, took one of her cigarettes, and lit it.

He walked into the living room and opened the liquor cabinet. The bottle of gin was in his hand, its delicate neck touched in indecision and guilt and then he let go and left it, shut the liquor cabinet and went over to the kitchen and opened the refrigerator.

There was a half-full bottle of white wine and he took it and pulled out the cork. Drinking from the bottle, he walked back to the bedroom, the cigarette still burning between his fingers. He sat down and drank.

The wine was cold but without freshness—sweet and effete—and the cigarette, with its slight flavor of mint, left him nugatory, as much as an invertebrate shadow.

The bed was there, unmade and empty, and he could hear the shower in the bathroom.

He put on the shirt and slipped his feet inside his boots, stuffing the socks in one jeans' pocket, then grabbed his jacket and walked out the door, the laces of his boots still undone. In silence he stepped outside and closed the door behind him, finding himself in an unfamiliar yard, and then walking out onto a street that he did not at first recognize.

He tied his laces and then walked down the road, the late morning sun extremely soft and the shadows of tree branches delicately patterned on the sidewalk.

97.

I carried my ice-chest with me stolen or mistaken for another's spicy chiffonade he naturally preferred knew what it was and though the last morning when we set out absolutely a butterfly counterfeit gourmet faces appear to flutter I might have taken it for a leaf but it had more charm good heels dragging and what not easy to cultivate could barely suck from a straw personally went her arms filling out her chair so we walked along helping cages containing Joe the Sky and Yekta followed behind with Ivan and Rusty doing my best to stay that way kinship to their hermaphroditic state to cross on my own I breathed or stop me because I meant to make it all the way and they stared Yekta laughing all the while and they stared not that they were feeling sorry but I think more like they were kind of scared at the sight of such a queer bunch as us.

That day though everybody must have been somewhere else because I don't remember cars coming, or else I did not see them because I was too busy paying attention to Servilia. I think I liked her an awful lot even though everybody was always making fun of me saying that Zahra was my girlfriend. But she was not. Even If I had wanted her to be, which I didn't, after what I saw Yves . . . well, I don't think it would have been right. Yves Hermite said, "Get out," and I got because I did not want to have anything to do with it. If I could have understood what Zahra was saying I would have asked her, but I can never understand a word of it, and I am not sure she can even understand me, though I think I am the best talker of the lot.

98.

1. The day had been long and banal.
2. Too like many other days.
3. Burying himself in the tomb of the mountains did not seem to add greatly to his pleasure.
4. To live again and again in memories, like some skeleton perpetually reanimated.
5. To live solely in recollections, those of missed and evaporated content, was a bit painful.
6. He scanned the array of canes set up against the wall of the vestibule, uncertain of which to take up in his hand and submit to the rigors of the earth outside.
7. Like Balzac, he too had a gold-knobbed walking stick.[1]
8. But there were many to choose from.[2]

----

1 It was of continental make, with a silver ferrule decorated with fleur de lis, a malacca shaft of gorgeous patina, and a brass finial, which, all be it somewhat battered, was not without charm, being the long variety used in the days of old, when walks through the mud were more or less a matter of course.

2 There was an American walnut cane dating from the revolution, the handle of antler, and an immense and crude ferule made

9. It was a habit of his never to use the same stick twice in a row.

10. Jae-yong picked up his eighteenth-century sword cane, with whalebone handle and platinum eyelets.

11. He weighed it in his hand.[1]

12. A million miles seem inches now.[2]

13. The telescope cane was out of the question.[3]

14. He smiled weakly as he handled the knob of the rare pistol cane.[4]

15. The flashlight cane?

16. No, the elegant walking stick from the roaring twenties would do; into the opera handle of which was concealed a cigarette lighter, and in the blackened bamboo shaft a vial of brandy.

17. He opened the door and stepped out into the dying light.

18. The sky was a deep blue and the air thoroughly still.

---

of iron. . . . It was more of a weapon than a tool of elegance; something one might savagely maul an enemy with. Next to this was one of his prizes, a simple oak cane unremarkable in all ways except that it had once been the primary companion on the jaunts of President Andrew Johnson.

1 No; he was not expecting to have a duel under the pines that evening; to skewer some enemy, wet the earth of the hill with revenged blood.

2 He had a walking stick which could be transmuted into a violin, but there was no party, heaving bosom mounted in a windowsill, presently available for him to serenade.

3 It would soon be dark, and it was an inadequate apparatus for star gazing, more fit to descry an invading Spanish galleon or two.

4 He had not the resolve to blow his brains out that evening.

19. Nighthawks flitted about, dark and shy shadows, gobbling up insects, disappearing into the silhouettes of the pines or the eaves of the house which sat somber and ghostly behind him, his haunting ground.

20. He set his cane and feet on the earth and traversed the path, which led away from the road and toward the quiet ridge that knew him.

21. The trail led along the edge of the mountain, a few legs of rock jutting off below him. The chirp of crickets issued from the bushes and the distant, corrugated horizon looked as if it were a thin streak of blood.[1]

22. He strode on.[2]

23. The lights of the town opened up below like the arms of a starfish.

24. The bright and bubbling vein of the highway dripped in from the southwest, sliced through the body of the town, and then veered northward, stripped of most of its life, a few flits of traffic making their way over the surge of hill.

---

1 He thought of Rimbaud's line, "Les courants de la lande," and how impressive the drama of nature was, with its massive gulfs, plains of bent, weeping grass, tortured sea-coasts, and the infernos called cities which sit like pots of thick and dangerous stew on the face of the globe.

2 Tracing the path with his stick and letting his eyes wander over the empty space to his left, where the drop gradually became more pronounced, and the rocks gathered up into cliff-face. They lipped up and formed a bastion, a line of defence along one side of the trail, and this terminated, along with the trail, in a suffusion of boulders and barren earth that rose up like the prow of a ship. He mounted this promontory, his figure silhouetted against the night sky as it disembroiled itself from the bleak shadow of the trees.

25. Jae-yong was grateful to have a place to sleep wedged amongst the trees in back of him.[1]
26. Inarticulate abbreviations of unclassified pain.
27. He extracted the cigarette case from his coat pocket and removed the last but one of the Turkish ovals.
28. After inserting the cylinder between his thin lips, he lifted the cane, and, with both thumb and forefinger, simultaneously opened the end of the opera handle and pulled the trigger of the lighter.
29. An eye of bluish-orange flame briefly exposed his face.
30. The rich smoke pressed down into his weary lungs and then poured out of his nostrils, two plumes, forthwith joining together and slowly rising into the night, the stars now twinkling overhead and the mountain permeated by the singularity of the void.
31. He felt sadder than he had in a great while.
32. He leaned on his cane and listened to the chirp of the crickets and observed the outline of the distant hills and the lights of far-away houses.
33. He stirred the small rocks and dirt beneath his foot and savored the fact that this pressure applied by his toe would not make the world yield.
34. Turning, he descended the little promontory and felt his way back along the trail.

---

1 He had done his time as a nomad, and treasured the simple comfort of a mattress, a blanket and a set of clean sheets.

99.

Two Americans sat side by side on the bicycle rickshaw in Old Delhi. They watched with weary eyes the young man before them, his naked back and strained legs, pushing down on the pedals.

The wheels rolled on into a section of town that tourists would only find themselves in by accident. The two remained mute. They were not tourists.

When their son's one-month vacation had turned into three without word from him, it became apparent that there was a problem. He had never boarded the return flight. His traveler's cheques had all been cashed within days of his arrival in New Delhi. No postcards. No telephone calls. Rusty was missing.

Dr. Maddox and his wife Margaret flew in to New Delhi and raised their voices at the United States Embassy, but were no better off. They went to Agra and Jaipur, and showed a blown-up photo around at all the hotels. A flight was taken to Benares. He was looked for along the banks of the Ganges. . . . At a burning ghat Margaret caught sight of the corpses being consumed by flames. The odor reached her nostrils and she fainted.

Rusty had mentioned the possibility of backpacking through the Northern country. Dr. Maddox and Margaret took themselves as far as Kashmir, consulting all the known guides, showing the photo at guesthouses and restaurants. Some suggested that he might have joined a religious community and gone into retreat, others said that he was most likely in jail. One young Israeli gravely informed them that they should expect the worst. . . . Their son could have easily fallen off a trail while traversing the steep hills. His remains might conveniently be concealed by the underbrush, the thick vegetation, or have been carried off by hungry monkeys.

Absolutely drained of both energy and emotion, the parents returned to Delhi to resume their investigation at the source. They posted, wherever permitted, flyers, offering a considerable sum in U.S. dollars for information leading to the whereabouts of Rusty. Dr. Maddox swore he would not leave the country without the boy. Inside, both the husband and wife despaired of ever seeing their progeny again.

One evening, returning to the Hilton hotel after a fruitless day, a man accosted them. He said that he had information which he believed to be pertinent to their cause.

100.

The street they arrived at seemed a little better than those in the immediate environs. It was uncrowded and sedate. The buildings appeared to be old bungalows gone to waste, mixed with a few newer structures in equal neglect.

"This must be it," Dr. Maddox said, indicating for the rickshaw driver to stop.

"Yes, he said it was a pink structure," murmured Margaret. "This is the only one."

They descended to the gate uneasily, leaving the rickshaw driver to sponge the sweat from his body with a gray strip of cloth.

Dr. Maddox banged at the gate, but no one came. He called out and presently a female form approached, the hand grasping a loose fold of sari and veiling an unattractive, pock-marked face. A voice clacked from behind the veil, abrasive, interrogatory, incomprehensible.

"Do you speak English?" Dr. Maddox demanded. "Is there anyone here who speaks English?"

"Fifty rupee."

"But . . ."

"Fifty rupee."

"I suppose that is all of our language she knows," said Dr. Maddox, handing her a bill.

"Fifty rupee," the voice demanded.

"Why, I've already given you——"

"Give her more money," Margaret said impatiently, taking the bankroll from her husband's hand and pushing it through the bars of the gate.

The money disappeared amidst the airy folds of garment, and the American couple was allowed to enter. A clenching hand motioned for them to follow, and they walked behind the bare brown feet, the overtly swaying hips.

Music could be heard, whiny, sorrowful, semi-ecstatic. A squat figure sat lumped on the porch, draped in sky-blue material, eyes, unsettlingly bold, staring forth. A fan waved before that morose, lardy face, the head nodded, lips pursed out a smile.

Through an opening and into an inner courtyard they were led. Figures, grouped in a circle, sitting, some leaning languidly back, bellows of colorful cloth, a tambourine jingling, a flute pressed to red slits, a glossy aperture. One stood singing, voice high, struggling, vibrating its way skyward, pitches flicked into the still, torpid air.

"It seems to be some kind of harem," muttered Dr. Maddox, his natural feeling of discomfort edging toward alarm.

The music came to a nearly abrupt halt, the tambourine's jingle trailing to a final point. The one who had led them pointed, declaring loudly, shortly, in

Hindi. One of the sordid figures stood up, turned its head away, two small breasts angling out the cloth. . . . First standing hip-shot, then, veiled, turning, advancing with a faltering, feminine gait.

Dr. Maddox had a distinctly queasy feeling, one he would not forget for many years, while he yet drew breath. His wife stared into the advancing eyes with morbid fascination. The fabric shielding the face dropped.

"You've found me," he said, in a voice they did not recognize, grown womanish, foreign.

The reunion was somber and strained. They invited him back to the Hilton hotel, but he refused.

"But you're coming home with us . . . no matter . . . you are still our . . . son," his mother said, tears gently melting down her cheeks.

"Yes," added Dr. Maddox. "There is . . . therapy back home. . . . The sacrificial tendency . . . just because of what . . ."

Rusty shook his head.

"This is my home now," he said. "These people, the eunuchs, understand me. . . . At first I rebelled, hated them for what was done. . . . But now I'm reconciled. . . . As much as I ever will be. . . . If I were still a man, I would look for a wife, have a family. If I were truly a woman, I would take a husband—I could have babies. . . . But now, though I am alive, you cannot claim . . ."

101.

Seeing me she trembled, her lips pouted. She was pretty. . . . Shaving I would think of her, purposely bury the razor deep . . . blood coloring the white soap suds, streaking down my face.

Some creatures ate away at my scalp. One drilled into my left temple. A pain flashed through the bulbs of my eyes. I could hear them buzzing. They were draining the blood from my brain.

At Diamond Head, Dustin was on duty. He served me drinks on the house. . . . Undoubtedly he had spiked the liquor . . . STP. . . . A woman sat next to me, a mound of beauty, a strange mishap.

Out of my mouth floated words, dropping like weights in space, logos of amour, sending spirals of emotion that lapped against the shore of her face and made it grimace. . . . Liquid flowed from my mouth.

Geeta . . . I still see you and long to clip open my feeble chest, pluck out my diminutive heart and serve it up to your lips on a platter of platinum. But I found myself immobilized. Men with thick hands held me, looked me over. I struggled. I strained my neck.

102.

"He is beautiful," she thought.

The situation was not putrid.

Claude looked at her gravely. He was obviously sensitive enough to guess.

Outside it was raining, dark and windy. A tree branch scratched at the window aggressively. She could imagine how the gutters seethed and, looking down at her own plump shoulders, rubbed her chin against one. She was in no rush to make a reply and enjoyed having Claude's eyes rest on her in subtle anticipation.

She did not dare think, think too much about it, but she could feel, could not help but feel. Men could pose and posture to their hearts' content, but she knew, Geeta knew, that for what she lacked men too would lack, would always wonder.

"And is there no one you love?" she asked.

"Myself. I love myself. Passionately."

Claude's features were exquisitely pale, burnt out, serene, cruel. He inspired respect and fear.

The door opened and Carsten ran in, his wet bangs plastered over his face. His eyes scanned the room.

"Oh, it's dry in here!" he said removing his dripping coat.

Claudia looked at him disdainfully.

Carsten sat down. He looked at Geeta but felt no sympathy for her.

As Geeta and Claudia sat near each other, he could not help but make comparisons.

Claudia was austere. Delicious. A nightmare. What was strange was in fashion. Her figure left much to the imagination. . . . Just as well. Something about her reminded him of a boyhood friend.

"Am I in your way?" she said, looking at Carsten.

"If I appear uncomfortable I can assure you that it is not because of you. There is not a thing that I could tell you or you could tell me that we do not already know."

"And Geeta?"

"Her have a secret!?!"

"We all have our secrets," said Claudia. "Some are simply pitiful, some are perverse."

Why should he, when it came down to it, tremble. . . . Everything would turn out when the time came, hopefully without violence or torture, but what of it if it were otherwise? Stars and sunbeams. The dissolution of dreams.

103.

The filth was there, lingering at the edge, but the tree-spotted hills became backed by a gray and soft light and the stars melted into the horizon. The way led toward the mountains. The piñons surrendered to larger pines which were still dark and the rising mountains did not let in the morning light. To his left a meadow opened up which was high with yellowing grass and olive-green mullein, whose velvety flowers were to him gross and reminiscent. There were deer which came in the morning to drink from the stream and on the surface he acknowledged them as they broke and ran. The light touched the top of trees high up on a ridge and, as he came around a bend, he saw the distant summit of the mountain, yellow with fall color. The car labored up, into the mountains, and the pine trees became interspersed with the changing aspens. A trail led off, through the trees, and he walked and felt the cool of the high altitude. There was the silence of silence and then the bird that sat perched deep in the shade of the forest cried out and the wind came from on high and blew through the trees. The way lay through the big shade-pines and the spindly, whitish-gray trunks of the aspens shone. In the small meadow, that the trail went down and through, there were wild geraniums, toad-flax and dandelions whose flowered heads were white. Stinging nettle grew toward the edge of the meadow and he walked through and beneath the tall trees, then down and into the lower forest.

CUT TO: A BEDROOM IN HERMOPOLIS. MEDIUM-SHOT OF SAMIR. DAY.
Samir is wearing a pair of jeans. He is shirtless and barefoot. He looks about him with a disconsolate expression, then, seeming to regain some level of vitality, opens up the drawer of a mock-oak nightstand. He pulls out the works, and, after preparing the substance and tapping the air bubbles out of the needle, drives the gleaming tip deep into his arm. His face is tightened up and concentrated on the act.

SPIRIT OF THE NEEDLE: The phallic significance.

VOICE OF DR. MADDOX: . . . due to the over-stimulation of the genitalia . . . and so the masculine organ begins to mimic various natural and unnatural phenomenon, such as trees, telephone poles and shovels . . .

CUT TO: GERMANY. COUNTRYSIDE. DAY.
"End of the World" by Aphrodite's Child plays on the soundtrack. We see men exhibiting themselves. Some drink beer, smoke cigarettes and laugh while engaging in deviant behavior. They bathe their bodies in the ice-cold creek while animals—dogs, cows, horses—watch.

CUT TO: UNITED STATES. DAY.

Jae-yong shuts the door of the car and stands listening. There is no sound except that of the cottonwoods down by the creek and the creek itself. The leaves rustle and then a bird sings from a branch. He looks over and sees the small bird shoot up from the yellowing fall foliage. It flies about and then descends into the branches of the cottonwoods and Russian olives further down the creek.

CUT TO: HEART OF THE AMAZON JUNGLE. DAY.

The last member of the Choénoé tribe sips water from a folded leaf. The violent sound of machinery can be heard in the background. The Choénoé looks up sadly, then rises to his feet. We see him, naked aside from his penis sheath, cross over a log bridge, then recede into the forest.

CUT TO: A WHITE ROOM WITHOUT FURNITURE. DAY.

The room is brightly lit with fluorescent lights. A brother and sister stand naked in the middle of the room. They are extremely blonde, with no pigmentation to their skin or hair. They look identical, the only difference between the two being that their sexual organs differ and the female has long hair and breasts. The two, without passion, begin to kiss and make love.

104.

So the building with its repertoire of nurses and medicines and treatments was left behind against a surge of rising blue hill. The two lean faces were positioned side by side, one aglow with mute rapture, the other, older, its jaw moving in monotonous and unhurried cadence: "The blood of both the night crawler and day worm are poison if taken in large doses, but with proper handling I will hook it onto the pin. The silver flash of the pin, combined with the writhing of the day worm, will attract the salmon which we will roast over an open blaze. You will not need to buy lunch. It will be my treat. You provide the beverages, friend, and I will provide the flesh. There is purity in the streams, friend. I will be careful not to slip on the mossy stones, because even in the depth of a spoon the intake of oxygen can be impaired. The bones and ligaments . . ."

"They've got it," Samir thought. "If I don't get over there, they are going to throw it away; they don't know what it is, they will just throw it away."

He arose from his seat, turned and walked down the isle, impervious to those pairs of visual apparatus which looked up at him in quiet and dull astonishment as he proceeded to turn the latch marked in red. The slab of door swung open, the whip of the wind pushing aside the bellowing and futile shouts, and there was that golden strand which squirmed alongside, trailing into the past, and over the hills filtered by shadow. There was that white post, motion, soft pillow and support and above the oblong open set like jewels mounted on a strawberry, his voice in the background, a hand pushing over the surface of a file, its tip could poke and make you cry; the ease of her breast fell away, he stepped out and into the crib which cracked.

CUT TO: NEW JERSEY STATE LUNATIC ASYLUM. DAY.
A large room painted red. There is no furniture, but various pieces of modern art placed around the space: abstract sculptures on pedestals, vibrant cubist paintings on the walls, etc. Three men stand, each in their own area of the room. They are wearing blue jumpsuits and their arms are outstretched.

MAN #1: I love her. Her cheeks were covered with numerous cavities, on the average each one being 1.36 mm in depth and averaging one every 0.96 cm on the fleshy portion covering the masseters her sternocleidomastoids were prominent making the depression below the trachea pronounced the orbicularis oculi showed darkening possibly due to lack of necessitated sleep though more probably from a natural inclination in the species towards manifold methods of intoxication radiating from the area above the parietal bone was a thick yet trimmed coating of hair speaking she spoke in slow deliberate tones.

MAN #2: After wine the maddest ideas occur. I saw in her a powerful angel; I would willingly prostrate on the ground and kiss her feet like a slave. Her proud looks both crushed and filled me with wonder. A cold shiver went up my spine.

MAN #3: I knew that I would make headway if I just stuck to my battle plan. I saw her fortifications weakening and then crossed the slender bridge of my wit. It took every ounce of my strength to retain composure. The finches had disappeared since morning. The cool trees with their bark humming with the sound of cicadas sighed in the form of the soft swishes of leaves. And what of it if deep in her heart lay the now infertile seed of some great romance that never had been? Her thin, rope-like waist with its little brown belly. Hot red spots, stripped of feathers and holes displaying fragile bone. Each man endeavors to be heard. Each woman refused to listen.

105.

"I woke up in the early hours of the morning."

"My mind was my feet watching not to step my voice so high and quick that I hardly knew it was mine."

"It was still dark out. It must have been three or four. My throat was totally dry and my feet felt like they were on fire."

"I could see the reflections of my arms moving wildly and as I walked up it turned into two faces that were me."

"The madness of the room demons mingled feelings I have an external staircase if they need it most muscular mountain."

"I leaned over and saw the smile on Jae-yong's face, so I went ahead and climbed in and looked out the window bouncing balls."

"I turned on the lamp at the bedside and looked down at my ankles."

"First of all, the error of judgment . . ."

"I suddenly became extremely frightened."

"I am in a broad field."

"I could see the clear sky of stars the upside down

of his spread legs and the long white finger spraying on me and it was over before I fully realized what that was doing."

"The Faction has limited powers."

"I thought of me and what I was and who I was and how I couldn't help it. I couldn't help it and it felt good and I couldn't help that. We were parked and then he started shooting at the crows. I could see puffs of feathers blooming off of them, then they would reel to the ground, but usually swoop up before they hit and make skyways again."

"The last male is behind me."

"Do you remember what happened seven years ago?"

"Well . . ."

"I rose out of bed, but immediately fell to the ground. I had no strength in my legs."

"Take for example the idea that we have equal portions . . ."

"I crawled toward the door . . ."

"For my part, I am not a fish. When I am alone in the house the place is enough. Night at last reigns over me, but I nod, then begin. I begin to dance, and find in the world another place. The forests in the liquid red with the blood of all the trees. Because it looks so unlike sex. I should have tried to explain the appearance of the neck. The tunic of skin. The pressure of the net."

"We left the car outside and walked in. There was just that long sweep that led up to it and plastic wrappers, torn paper and packaging blew around. A lot of useful things were scattered and I picked some of them up thinking that they might come in handy or I could sell them. There was old furniture that I would have put in my house if I had one, and even without one I saw a chair that might have looked nice down by my grate."

"The lick of flame mirroring in his eyes and then snapped up by the night I smelled the aroma scooping up those leavings rising in the air towards the dots in the sky his face red."

"Don't blame me, people, don't blame me!"

"Blood flowed freely."

"I wish I could sing."

"To roar."

106.

I realized full well that, though I had but little strength, now was the time to exert it if I hoped to see the light of day again. I could not imagine the Duke setting me free after what I had seen, heard and experienced at his hands. For, bound, I might, out of necessity, accept degradation; but free, I could never forgive it and, on my honor, only wash it away in the rivulet of his shed blood.[1]

Straining myself to the utmost, by the power of my arms, which was by no means slight, I pulled my head up to the level of my encumbered wrists. I grappled the rope with my jaws, trying to imagine the fibers as the sweetest cake which I need must masticate.[2] Three times

---

1 The two henchmen; the torchlight glowing on their sodden faces, a jug of strong spirits poised between them. I grabbed it up and cracked it over Mullo's skull. The brute awoke with a cry, well drenched in liquor. Taking the torch from the wall with one hand, I stabbed his startled companion in the belly with the other. Mullo rushed towards me, his face drooling blood. I flung the torch upon him, igniting his features and, with a kick to his chest, sent him sprawling back.

2 His companion lay bleeding on the floor, not yet dead. I took his sword from him, from its sheath, and dispatched him, sending

I pulled myself high, and three times made a meal of the rope, with each successive effort my arms and jaws growing more exhausted, though exhausted I was from the outset, in a measure I have never before nor since experienced. A fourth time I made the strain, clasped the rope in my jaws and chewed with mad frenzy. I plied my wrists. The ropes broke and I fell to the floor. My head was feverish, my body coated shiny with an unclean sweat. The immediate mobility of my parts, however, lent renewed energy to my frame.

The Duke's sheathed dagger sat within the pile of his cast-away clothes. I reached the object and drew it glittering out.

The Duke it was who I had every reason to consider the most dangerous of the party. I saw him lying upon his rabbit furs, one arm thrown back behind his head. I approached him and cut open his white throat till the blood boiled forth like a spring. His eyes opened wide. He tried to give utterance to his discomposure and I, well understanding his predicament, smiled while I saw him die, but they kept on tossing stuff that hit me in the head[1] and it felt like it might have cracked my head and the pain went back over all the way behind one ear and his mother was next and I did so with the utmost joy and it would not be handsome of me to brag of the just mutilation she endured, but let it be known that

---

his head rolling down the hall.

[1] The Baroness was next. I approached her and saw that she was awake. Her frame quaked; her timid eyes stared up at me, with tender supplication. I slipped the blade through her supple neck with a grace her distinction deserved.

I left her well punctured, in an ever-widening puddle of gore and dispatching snoring Rogero was an act of but a moment as I severed the perverse manikin's head from his shoulders and tossed it aside and down the hall naked flecked and smeared with blood I skipped up the stairs feeling the cold stones beneath my feet.

107.

THERE'S A LIVE ANIMAL ON MY HEAD AND
IT'S DRIPPING MILK SOFTLY RIPPING OFF
THE EAR AND EAT IT UNDER TORTURE
FUCKING FROTHING LIQUID MOUNTING
THINK BROWN COWS HOT LIFE LEAVING
LONG VINES OF ENTRAILS OVER THE
BLACK SKY AND IMPOTENT AIR LIKE THE
CASTRATED PRIEST I AM THE WOMAN THE
FIRE AND THE WATER THE EARTH AND THE
SEAT MASSAGING BEARDS AND TRUCKS
OF LARD YOU IMPIOUS SPIT SHE SPIT SPIT
HUNG SPIT FELL AND CLOUDS CAME FROM
HIS THROAT HAUNTING AS GHOULS AND A
CRUEL THRILL RAN THROUGH HIM GROP-
ING AND OOZING I CLENCHED MY TONGUE
BETWEEN MY TEETH AND YOU CRAWLED
OUT OF ME AND NOW STAND NAKED ON
ONE LEG IN ELEPHANT SHIT THINKING OF
BEDROOM DOORS.

108.

fire-flies
sunsets
wombs, warmth
unclear and jittery
sodium pentothal
potassium chloride twisted its way through the plastic
tube

CUT TO: EXTREME CLOSE-UP OF JAE-YONG'S
EYES.

CUT TO: MUZHI, RUSSIA. HEADQUARTERS
OF THE METAL SEVENS GROUP.
*Maksim Bezrukov, group leader, stands before his disciples,
of which there are around twenty. He is dressed in a thick
fur coat. His fingers are covered with rings and a thick gold
chain with an odd gold medallion hangs from his neck.*

MAKSIM BEZRUKOV: And so, if a man does not
    engage in regular genital activity, he will soon take
    on the traits of the female—her gait, mannerisms,

tone of voice. Soon he will begin to dress as one. His beard will fall from his face. He will begin to speak of things such as his emotions and he will never be in an excellent mood.

CUT TO: INTERIOR. SAN QUENTIN. A HALL. MOVING SHOT OF JAE-YONG'S FEET WALK-ING. NIGHT.
We see Jae-yong's feet walking. They are manacled and one of the pant-legs is cut away. That leg is shaven. He wears slippers.

CUT TO: EXTERIOR. ICELAND. DAY.
A huge crowd of men, thousands, all very pale and completely naked, run frantically towards the waters edge and throw themselves in.

CUT TO: STOCK SHOTS OF HIPPOPOTOMI, LIONS AND MONKEYS.
In slow motion we see the animals in their natural environments, the wilds of the natural world. Monkeys in trees, lions on the savanna, hippopotami bathing and splashing in deep waters.

CUT TO: STOCK SHOT OF ANDY WARHOL'S *ELECTRIC CHAIR.*

CUT TO: FULL SHOT: THE EXECUTION ROOM.
We see the chamber of execution. A chair similar to that at a dentist's office sits amidst the tools for lethal injection.

EXTREME CLOSE-UP OF JAE-YONG'S FACE.
We see Jae-yong's face. It is terror-stricken.

EXTREME CLOSE-UP OF JAE-YONG'S HAND.
*We see Jae-yong's hand. It is being strapped into the chair
with leather straps. It struggles desperately.*

CLOSE-UP OF JAE-YONG'S HEAD.
It writhes in the chair, yanking from side to side.

STOCK SHOT OF ANDY WARHOL'S *ELECTRIC
CHAIR.* RED. YELLOW. GRAY. PINK. RED.

GREEN. RED.

GREEN.

A PARTIAL LIST OF SNUGGLY BOOKS

FREDERICK ROLFE (**Baron Corvo**) *Amico di Sandro*
FREDERICK ROLFE (**Baron Corvo**)
An Ossuary of the North Lagoon and Other Stories
JASON ROLFE *An Archive of Human Nonsense*
BRIAN STABLEFORD (**editor**)
Decadence and Symbolism: A Showcase Anthology
BRIAN STABLEFORD (**editor**) *The Snuggly Satyricon*
BRIAN STABLEFORD *The Insubstantial Pageant*
BRIAN STABLEFORD *Spirits of the Vasty Deep*
BRIAN STABLEFORD *The Truths of Darkness*
COUNT ERIC STENBOCK *Love, Sleep & Dreams*
COUNT ERIC STENBOCK *Myrtle, Rue & Cypress*
COUNT ERIC STENBOCK *The Shadow of Death*
COUNT ERIC STENBOCK *Studies of Death*
MONTAGUE SUMMERS *The Bride of Christ and Other Fictions*
GILBERT-AUGUSTIN THIERRY *The Blonde Tress and The Mask*
GILBERT-AUGUSTIN THIERRY *Reincarnation and Redemption*
DOUGLAS THOMPSON *The Fallen West*
TOADHOUSE *Gone Fishing with Samy Rosenstock*
TOADHOUSE *Living and Dying in a Mind Field*
RUGGERO VASARI *Raun*
JANE DE LA VAUDÈRE *The Demi-Sexes and The Androgynes*
JANE DE LA VAUDÈRE *The Double Star and Other Occult Fantasies*
JANE DE LA VAUDÈRE *The Mystery of Kama and Brahma's Courtesans*
JANE DE LA VAUDÈRE *The Priestesses of Mylitta*
JANE DE LA VAUDÈRE *Syta's Harem and Pharaoh's Lover*
JANE DE LA VAUDÈRE *Three Flowers and The King of Siam's Amazon*
JANE DE LA VAUDÈRE *The Witch of Ecbatana and The Virgin of Israel*
AUGUSTE VILLIERS DE L'ISLE-ADAM *Isis*
RENÉE VIVIEN AND HÉLÈNE DE ZUYLEN DE NYEVELT
Faustina and Other Stories
RENÉE VIVIEN *Lilith's Legacy*
RENÉE VIVIEN *A Woman Appeared to Me*
KAREL VAN DE WOESTIJNE *The Dying Peasant*